You Could Live
If They Let You

You Could Live

Wallace

Alfred A. Knopf

If They Let You

Markfield

New York 1974

THIS IS A BORZOI BOOK
PUBLISHED BY ALFRED A. KNOPF, INC.

Library of Congress Cataloging in Publication Data

Markfield, Wallace.   You could live if they let you.

I. Title.
PZ4.M3453YO   [PS3563.A664]   813'.5'4   74-8373
ISBN 0-394-46056-1

Manufactured in the
United States of America

First Edition

For the wisest men of our time—
the stand-up comics

You Could Live
If They Let You

1

"This is me?"
"It's you, it's you!"

A tummler by instinct, Jules Farber gives the impression that he is leading us all to the Grossinger's pool for a fast game of Simon Says, that beset and beleaguered simultaneously by all the drives, he is obeying only one—the Israel Bond Drive.

Albert Manchester, New York Magazine

He saw America, I believe, as a vast shtetl with 220-volt wiring. . . .

Herbert Sundel, The Villager

Admittedly, Jules Farber was a gifted and, at times, even a brilliant parodist. And there are some amongst us who call him genius and heir to the tradition of Sholom Aleichem, who claim that a few gentle gibes at our American Jewish Community and its institutions are healthy and all to the good. Yet I for one am saddened and made sorrowful by the negative and self-hating qualities of his work. Indeed, I cry shame and fie upon him for routines—I think principally of one which implies that a Jewish President would fail to live up to the very highest standards demanded by that great office—which, for the sake of a cheap laugh, debase sixty years of human relations effort.

Rabbi A. Sigmund Lilyveld, *Jewish World Monthly*

What you should do—this is what you should do: Sublet the city to Polish groupies!

Jules Farber to Mayor John V. Lindsay
on "The Tonight Show"

Comics, before they are permitted to pass into camp ground—I think to some extent of W. C. Fields and Lenny Bruce—must suffer a sea change. Despair is downgraded to aggravation; madness is misread as eccentricity; and when from the extremes of alienation they rage and rail at us we hear or choose to hear a puny, pathetic cry for love. But worse, even, is the intellectual's habit of exalting them to the stature of prophets and gurus, of searching their work for commentary on the human condition, for a definition of the problems of our country and our culture.

Admittedly, I am tempted in this introduction to the works and ways of Jules Farber to "place" and "pigeonhole" him, to enlarge private perception into doctrine. For the herd of independent minds is already rediscovering and legendizing him, a scant year after his death, into a kind of apocalyptic Harry Golden or an acidulous Sam Levinson; some see him as the American Céline, as another—"only another"—example of that special Jewish genius for turning pinpricks into bloodbaths; and one observer believes him to have been placed on earth to punish B'nai Brith's Anti-Defamation League.

All agree, though, in this: Jules Farber was funny, wonderfully funny, and I shall try here only to suggest what qualities made him so funny, so wonderful, and to give some sense of these qualities and of the man himself whom I came, unbelievably, to know.

If I say "unbelievably" it is because I am an academic and,

given Farber's contempt for all academics ("*Yentas* with facts," he once called them), I had little reason to believe, in 1971, that he would grant me a meeting, perhaps even several meetings, to tape his thoughts on modern comedy and comedians.

I think, or perhaps I prefer to think, my letter engaged his interest because I presented myself at the outset as "an apple-cheeked, dewy-eyed *goy* who had the good fortune to have been adopted by a group of tough-minded New York Jewish intellectuals and taught how to think, to talk and to insist that my egg creams be served only in chilled glasses." In short order I received from him a note in which he (1) expressed the hope that I would one day purchase for companionship and the facilitation of certain odd sexual procedures a hypertensive parrot who would demand only salt-free crackers; and (2) granted me an appointment provided I would fill out and send along this statement:

I, Chandler Van Horton, do absolve Jules Farber of the killing of Christ. It is my understanding that the very worst his people might have done was to lean on Him a little.

Our first meeting, I now realize, must surely have coincided with that period which Buddy Hackett was to speak of as "a lousy, a miserable, a really fucked-up time" for Farber; there were holes in his life and he was falling through: Farber's career was not going badly, yet it was far from flourishing; he had made bad investments; insofar as a parent ever can "accept" it he had accepted the fact of his young son's autism; and he would before long suffer the dirtiness and damage of divorce.

All the same, neither he nor his home reflected any of this, and both were in a state of decent middle-class order. His cottage, in fact, was pure, perhaps too-pure Malibu—airy and glassy and insecurely perched on its steep little sandhill. But the Farberesque touch, that singular blend of joyous irreverence and brutal abrasiveness, revealed itself in the door chimes which at my touch triggered the voice of Cantor Lavbeleh Waldman in a ballad I had first heard sung by my good friend, Professor Daphne Cohen, and what follows is her translation from the Yiddish: *A drinker is he/ A drunkard must be/ For he is a goy.* Then, dour and suspicious, Farber admitted me, offering a quarter if I would mop his stoop and another quarter if I would return in advance of the Jewish Sabbath to fire his stove and turn on his night-light.

Somehow, though, I was not bothered by this, no more than the housekeeper—an elderly black lady lethargic and destructive in her movements—seemed to be bothered by Farber's threat to beat her with fat copies of *The Watchtower.* For she must surely have discerned, as I did, that if Farber was not exactly loving he was nonetheless likable. Admittedly, I might have been and might still be mistaken since we all of us tend as a matter of smug course to insist upon a comic's good nature, upon his essential sweetness and benevolence; the idea that a Don Rickles might even for five fast minutes wish us genuine harm would be unbearable. We laugh, then, as I laughed, willingly, fearfully, when Farber came at me with "I would offer you something, but what can I offer a *goy?* I only have in the house good food. . . ." He several times spoke my name ("That's a name or an intersection?") and for a tense time called me "Xavier" on the grounds that "all *goyim* are anyway Irish."

While I set up my cassette (I had trouble, which seemed to please him; he muttered, at any rate, "The English were right about you people") he several times sought to place a long-distance call, then took a turn about the room, touching in an oddly impersonal way the huge Chinese vases, the vents of the air conditioner, flicking on and off a master switch for heavy, handsome table lamps built to the scale of old movie palace lounges, once, even, sniffing the rich leather of a hassock—seeking, I felt, not to exhibit these objects as much as to exact what they owed him. (Jan Murray has claimed that Farber regarded all of California as one vast motel which was overcharging him: "I had the feeling he wanted to steal his own towels.")

Behaving like Old Man Karamazov, read my notes covering the next several minutes, *or like King Saul.* For he had started suddenly to shake both fists at the phone, to fling himself from chair to chair, his head sinking between his knees like one who concentrates on not fainting. Before too long he was overtaken by an ecstasy of aggravation, uttering suffering sounds, alternately begging and raging in disjointed phrases. "Go, go" . . . "Run, fly, hide" . . . "Busy, keep busy, you bubbleheads, you wild nutsy old creatures" . . . "Plan ahead, work it out, oh make sure, absolutely sure not to be in when he calls" . . . "My free spirits, there, my free souls, my glorious golden-agers."

But he was all smiles when the phone rang, answering with a "Mrs. Farber, do I have Mrs. Farber? Dr. Pincus Who-Gets-Fifteen-Hundred-Just-To-Open-You-Up here. Don't worry if your Jules sounds a little weak, this is only to be expected, we expect these things, the fourth heart transplant will sometimes take it out of you. Anyway it's not about that I'm calling, I'm calling about his dandruff; we ran a routine biopsy of one of the flakes. . . ." Then he listened and listened with his eyes squeezed shut as though quelling tears, grinning and mugging and taking little twirling steps. From high in his throat he half-crooned, half-growled senseless syllables of adoration; my knowledge of Hasidism is limited, yet I thought at the time that in this manner a Hasid must improvise messages to heaven. But presently he was back in character, teasing and bantering, though his voice was filled with a loving gruffness, evoking, perhaps for my benefit, an image, a suggestion at least, of the life his parents lived and the style in which they lived it.

There were references, at any rate, to Miami Beach—to Collins Avenue and Lincoln Road and Burdine's and Wolfie's. Something unpleasant, perhaps more than unpleasant, had evidently transpired at The Clubhouse (a sense of portentousness in Farber's tones accounts for my capitalization), and I could discern that he was cajoling first his mother, then his father, working to minimize what seemed to be his parents' genuine enough grief. Though Farber's

Yiddish was too stormy, too explosive for my untrained ear
(only the continued repetition of the sometimes ironic,
sometimes heartsick "*Azoi*" stayed with me), I gathered that
a good, a dear dear friend had refused his mother the loan
of a pencil—a Mark Cross pencil—on the grounds that it was
part of a matched, initialed and gold-filled set given by her
grandchildren; and this friend would not "risk the chance
that somebody should wet the tip." Whereupon Farber began hollering coarsely—not "gagging" or in any way dissem-
bling; I am convinced he was for the moment altogether
caught up in his parents' humor and implicit values—and
derisively, desperately charging his mother with continually
courting and catering to these types ("Negative personalities" . . . "Self-haters" who would not even Martinize their
furs). He several times repeated the phrase "Good for you!,"
recapitulating his mother's dealings with this harridan (so,
at least, I would translate *yochna*): How his mother had
eased the way for this "total unknown"; how she had "popu-
larized" her at pool-side; how she had exalted her from "not
even a canasta standby" to a "five-game regular"; how she
had sponsored her for the "group therapy group."

Strangely, there was no formal goodbye—only a whispered,
prayerful admonition to "Stay well, be well, keep well," followed by the blowing of a long kiss into the mouthpiece.
His lips still keeping the shape of that kiss, he proceeded to
prance and caper and was in no time delivering or being
delivered of a manic monologue, the main thrust of which
is herein set down. . . .

"Now, maybe now first you're ready for it—the whole
Jewish mystique and *meshugass*. The secret of our tenacity,
our survival. Yeah yeah! Because don't you think we could
have converted? We didn't have opportunities? We had
plenty opportunities. In fact it was arranged, it was all set up
and we were practically signing with Torquemada. But we
backed out; we had to back out. Because he wouldn't let us
call our mothers. Which is very important to us. *Vei*, is it

important! If you went to Jerusalem you'd see my people at the Wailing Wall—and what are they wailing? '*Oi*, I have to call my mother, *oi*, I should call my mother. . . .' You take a Moses; sure Moses wandered around forty years. Till he could find a phone . . . !"

Then, while he was needling me about my beard ("Enjoy it, because next week it's going to be registered with the State Department"), his housekeeper peeped in to announce that she would be off shopping; was there something special he wanted her to pick up? "A nice gonorrhea," he told her. To which she replied with a simple "Zionist imperialist." The singularity of their relationship struck me with some force, and I could not help but remark upon it—seeking to learn why he would keep so obvious an anti-Semite in his employ. "Because," he answered, "she *is* an anti-Semite." Taking pleasure in my bafflement—"With you they didn't include batteries"—he set out with spirited gravity, with an air of scholarly detachment, to develop a series of peculiar and (to me) provocative notions about Jewish destiny as it related to demography.

A Jew, he maintained, tended to lose his "sense and sensibility" (I am rendering Professor Cohen's equivalent for *saychel*) in direct proportion to the distance he placed between himself and the primary sources of anti-Semitism in the urban East. For if the anti-Semite needs the Jew, the Jew has almost as much need of the anti-Semite, whose function is to remind him that he must never cease to *tsitter*. ("*Tsitter* is . . . It's a Jewish euphemistic locution to imply—it implies an attitude, a state of mild concern; my people *tsitter* over children, your people *tsitter* over hay crops.") Without his *tsitter* the Jew is bereft of his special edge, his personal style, his flavor, his savor. Till he becomes— to some extent in Chicago, more so in Denver and absolutely in Los Angeles—a creature of bland, fatuous *Gemütlichkeit*, a Mr. Nonsectarian. ("Twenty years already he and his wife are learning how to mispronounce schmaltz . . . and they're very big in the Community Center. For Jewish Book Week they bring down Barry Gray; he gives readings from Max Lerner.")

Well, then, he would seem, I ventured, to be suggesting that a Jew should limit his experiences—to the eastern seaboard in general and New York City in particular. With this he agreed. ("When you're right you're right.") Whereupon I called his attention to a basic anomaly: Namely, he had himself left New York City. And I observed that he might have been obeying that inner necessity Hazlitt perceived in many a comic artist—a certain deliberate willing of, indeed, a tropism for, alienation.

His "Nah!" very nearly misted my glasses. He gave me to understand, rather, that epic struggle and *de profundis* had marked his every movement in New York City; his description of flagging down a cab, of having a pair of trousers cuffed or buying a container of milk late at night took on the proportions of the *Iliad,* and mere survival in that infernal metropolis called for the strength of Gilgamesh and Beowulf, the craft and cunning of Talleyrand. Everyone, he implied, sought with all his might to shine and put himself forward. ("You know the joke, 'Waiter, what time is it?' And he answers, 'I'm not your waiter.' Now ask him for the time, he tells you, 'God is love.'")

But all this and more he would have withstood. "Who cared and who minded?" No, what finally drained Farber of will and nerve was, if I understood him rightly, his apprehension that the culture of the city and the creators of that culture had fallen victim to a *meshugass:* an obsession with "one theme, one topic, one topic and one theme."

"You'd go into the Puerto Rican night . . . Upper Broadway . . . a living room with women. Women? A masthead, a panel, a symposium of poetesses, painters, philosophes scaling the Tibetan heights of consciousness, contending, creating, worrying how they should save the race. They're in the middle of inventing a new religion, a new civilization when all of a sudden . . .

" 'Did you hear that my diamond, my jewel, my Moses, my Leonardo, my sage, my savior, was just accepted at the Ethical Culture School?' "

"*School!*

"And right away the nostrils twitch, the nipples harden.

"*School!*

"Oh, what they're going through, oh, oh, what they've been through. And the stories, the sagas—an anthology of abominations.

"How they had to kick their mothers to death. 'I begged her, Ma, Ma, will you please hold still, you're not holding still, I didn't know you'd be such a lousy grandmother, just once more, Ma, a good one, I have to pulverize you in the pelvic girdle and he'll be on the Dalton waiting list.' How they had balled apes. 'Did I understand you, dear? Dear, what did you gibber? Something about the Montessori Method?' How they paid through the nose and every available orifice. 'Nine hundred and fifty was just for the *application*.' How they had been tested. 'She said my urine is too cloudy to admit him this year, but maybe if I cut down on the cholesterol. . . .' "

I observed, as Farber continued his narrative, that he would move in a wholly unmediated way from parody to paranoia. Thus, it is likely the brownstone ("the gallstone") he had renovated was vandalized, perhaps, indeed, "more often than Rome"; I take a dim view, however, of his claim that the vandals would leave behind notes apologizing for "de mess" and listing the telephone number "fo a nice quiet girl, $3.95 the hour, she iron good, no winders." (Farber's "kiss-a-pinkie" avowal, moreover, that the local doormen were forced to walk fighting cocks puzzled his sister, Mrs. Lillian Federman, who could remember nothing untoward about the neighborhood—save, perhaps, the absence of a Waldbaum's Supermarket and "once in a while a burning mattress.")

For as it turned out, he had as many complaints against California. The ocean—we had by then moved onto the sun deck—neither chilled nor warmed, neither gave off nor received color, neither moved nor stayed still, neither alarmed nor soothed by its sounds, neither was it smelly or odorless. Sand, surf, breeze were without qualities—and so, too, he implied, were the people. People? No, fair, smooth androids made of milk and gold, but essentially unfeeling—"the look on their faces, like they're reading meters!"—they represented a new race, if not a new life-form altogether, one that had been most likely created in some Kraft kitchen. Did he, then, consider them evil? By no means; in point of fact they were the quintessence of graciousness, good souls who thought nothing of changing your tire, cashing your checks, boosting your battery; knock on any California door, he asserted, and you would be permitted to piss and shit in the toilet. God bless their garage sales, the swift water of their sprinklers, the iron stags at bay on their lawns. Let His grace give relish to their cookouts, let the English coach lamps in their windows be lighted and their Japanese wind bells tinkle till the coming of the Messiah. And if nothing gave them so much pleasure as burning leaves, why they should live and be well and burn only leaves. But beneath their smiling teeth—a soul with smiling teeth. Unknowable and in stuporous sleep. Scratch at it, beat upon it—

—And Farber very suddenly sauntered to the railing, flung up his arms and unloosed a great-voiced "Gevald!" followed by "I'm alone like a stone" and "I got a terminal case of aggravation." And he next instructed me to wait and see what might follow. I can report only that the beach population continued its business of pleasure; at the very most, and I am not altogether certain, a young girl might have smiled and saluted with her frisbee.

While I silently debated between quoting Auden (*Each in the cell of himself . . .*) and D. H. Lawrence (*"The American soul is hard, stoic, isolate and essentially a killer"*) Farber explained how his notion, his vision, of the Californian had been planted in him. Returning by plane from Miami after attending the funeral of a distant relative—who had died, he gave me to understand, under the most blessed circumstances ("In a movie house, watching for the eleventh time *Fiddler on the Roof*")—he ran into some trouble at the airport. The limousine service people had gone on strike, few cabs were in sight and those few fiercely contested. He ended up, finally, sharing a ride with, as he saw her, a typical, an archetypal California matron: "babushka, rollers in the hair and an off-pink orlon cardigan tied off at the throat." Rain was falling, and a small amount of water leaked through the windshield. "American cars," the woman commented, then announced that she had no use for a Detroit product; indeed, her second Mercedes-Benz was on order. And why not? The Germans and the Germans alone built with integrity, with strict standards of quality control; they *crafted* their cars. Immediately the driver, a coarse strong compact little chap, pounded seat, steering wheel, brow, and in the purest Yiddish instructed her to, amongst other things, use the open sea for a chamber pot. Uncomprehending, the woman rattled on, praising all things German, unto the cigarette lighter which—she had demonstrated—flamed up at the first flick. "Yeah yeah" and "Sure sure" cried the driver; for his part Germany could be consumed by one fire. Of course there had been excesses during the war; but which nation, demanded the woman, was guiltless? Look, further, at what our own country, our own state had perpetrated upon its Japanese citizens. And she took scant notice of the driver who was by now relating how in Dachau certain sordid surgical procedures had been carried out upon his person, saying only that in these matters it was best to take the long view and the broad view; anyway she could if she chose find sufficient, more than sufficient to carp at in American medical practices. Emotionally, the driver informed her that he had weighed twenty-eight kilos (a bit more than sixty-one pounds) upon his liberation, that, further, it had taken two years before he could properly

walk and nearly three till he shook off the effects of a virulent
infection. To which the woman replied mildly, blissfully,
"Yes, yes, but you look fine now. . . ."

Who can say even now whether this was truth or trav-
esty—whether, in fact, it was not the kind of cold, iron-
hard epiphany which Farber favored and which at its best
lets us know perhaps as much as we can bear to know about
Americans: what they are, what they have become. I had at
the time several questions in mind, but while I struggled to
bring them forth Farber, with an inward, meditative look,
with his body at complete rest in a captain's chair, rattled
me by likening my expression to that of a "day-old *chalah*"
(the traditional celebratory Jewish twist) and demanded to
know if I had heard a piece of bad news from my Irish
meshpuchah. (In this context Professor Cohen prefers
"clan" to "family.") "Maybe the Wonder Bread shipment
didn't reach Dublin yet?" I had also to tell him what I
taught: Two sections of a seminar entitled "Maladies of
Modern Civilization," so loosely structured that I found
detailed description difficult. Whereupon Farber, crying
"Wait, wait!" announced that the course—"The course is
. . . it's a sweeping survey of modern man's struggle for
identity in a hostile cosmos . . . Readings from Kierke-
gaard, Kafka and Julia Child will be considered in an effort
to show how *Gemeinschaft* got displaced by *Gesellschaft*,
how *Homo faber* turned into *Homo laborans*"—I cannot,
alas, reproduce his explosive Chaucerian sounds—"with special attention to the rise, the emergence of mass man whose
notion of self, his self-notion has been eclipsed by the belief
that he is bereft of a share in the world. Right? Am I right?"

I had to concede that, if not altogether accurate, he was
certainly close enough to what was set down in the catalogue.

"Then first you register and it turns out to be—you know
what it turns out to be?" Farber cried. "Corrective Gym!"

My reply—a faltering defense of the academic structure
—carried overtones of acerbic self-righteousness. But Farber,
who could have demolished me entirely, easily, was just then

engaged with his housekeeper. (In the midst of desultory dusting she began muttering, "Hey, Leroy, wut de difference tween a Joo-ish coed and a submarine?" "Dunno, ain't never been in no submarine.") I sought to fill the silence that followed with a few nervous questions: Where did he get most of his material? ("From an unmarked truck.") How would he rate the work of, say, Alan King, Buddy Hackett or Jackie Mason? ("Not Jewish enough.") Thereupon he stopped me, calling me *goyishe kopp* and instructing me to "make a little human relations."

And I soon perceived that I was to him an object of supreme curiosity—part Penrod, part Andy Hardy, part, certainly, Caliban. For he began improvising on themes from some mythical, monstrous Middle-American boyhood, conjuring up a *"shkutzy* shtetl" compounded of Dr. Pepper and ham hocks and fish fries and snowmobiles and pickup trucks and Rotary Club bake-offs where lumpen lugs joined on American Legion bowling nights to talk of trailer hitches and creeping socialism. Here, between nothing and nowhere ("There's no place to go but when you get there they give you plenty of parking"), he had me coming of age. (At nineteen months uttering my first sentence: "Trouble at the mill!") And he begged and baited me to tell him what, precisely what it was like to be a *goy*, one of the managers, nay—the owners of America. Was I handy with fists and tools? Did I know the names of flowers and herbs? Had my mother risen with or among roosters to prepare, before she went off to her shift at the foundry, fantastic fatty meals, perking pot after pot of real coffee? (Only the Jews, he believed, drank instant: "That's why the Egyptian soldiers yell across the Suez, 'Down with Nescafé. . . .'") Would she worry over my very last cell and secretion, kissing my "doodoo and my poopoo and my voovoo?" Celebrating my tiniest triumphs? ("Not because he's mine, but with three matches he kin burn down the biggest barn.") Or was she dry, spare, neutral, rearing me with typical *"shkutzy* stoicism?" ("A mite touch polio is all.") My father—what of my father? Had he been a ballsy brute of a man icily indifferent to his eighteen children—each of whom had a different vitamin deficiency—given to wearing a tiny peaked hat of Howard Johnson orange ("his tailgating hat")? A stern disciplinarian? ("Maybe when ye finish drainin' the leech field ye'll remember tuh call me 'Sir'. . . .") Accepting, with his kind's unthinking conviction, the world as it was given him? The pleasures it could afford him? ("An annual fire-hose festival, a brewery tour, a pig gelding, once a week a box of Fanny Farmer mixed creams or a milk shake at Dairy Queen. . . .") Oh, and guns. Did he make a move without a gun? ("The way my people carry shopping bags your people carry guns. . . .")

And as he built and built the case against me and my kind, as he held me under the beam of his bloodshot eyes, I had the momentary notion that I could not merely sense but see, almost literally see his rage—his helpless, miserable abominable, ulcerous rage. For it hung upon him like some bodily effusion, like a *Doppelgänger*. I could not, I would not think too long of how it must have been sustained; I wanted no further insight into those sources which fed and fevered it. Was I a Roman, a Crusader, a Mameluke, a Cossack to be borne down by the weight of that stockpile, that five-thousand-year inventory of memory? Enough, more than enough, I wanted to say: Remember, please, you are dealing with a *goy*, a liberal, a *goyishe* liberal who is younger than you in history, one who has the training and temperament to go so far and so far only. . . .

Then to stop his maddening monologue—he was fantasying my family's shopping list: a quarter-pound of ground muskrat meat, one frankfurter, a make-your-own-margarine kit, three factory reject cans of Campbell's tomato soup, a jar of Jane Parker marshmallow-and-lard spread, a giant box of Hong Kong sanitary napkins and an aerosol tube of garbage cleanser ("The *goyim* love to clean their garbage") —I moaned a Farberesque moan. Following this and in keeping with his style, my hands described arcs, spheres, parabolas, grabbing at straws or lapels in the air, cupping glasses of tea. "*Oi*," I cried, tearing at my breast as though to expose a hair shirt, "do I need this? I don't need this. . . ." Whereupon Farber broke into a heavy, liquidy laugh and emitted what seemed to me an admiring "*Azoi!*"

"Look here," I declared, "if I can forgive your people their Mah-Jongg I think you can forgive mine their soft ice cream. I am not Middle America, you are not Levittown. If the milk shake is not the repository of the higher wisdom, neither is the egg cream."

While he protested ("Our ritual baths are better than your saunas" . . . "Moses Maimonides could beat up Thomas Aquinas". . . "We gave you Exodus, you gave us the U-Haul") I pressed on with an account of my parents. My mother, I informed him, had been a Colorado State Senator who had put some thirty-five thousand miles on the odometer of her converted hearse to petition against dismissal of three devoutly Reichian schoolteachers. She was—I could not resist hectoring him with this—a superb, a gourmet cook; named for her were a poached fish sauce, two salad dressings and a summer squash pie. Apart from rearing three children passably well she had been—indeed, still was—a serious photographer, a cellist in a highly praised string quartet and the author of one of the basic texts on organic gardening. If anything more was needed, my mother, at the age of fifty-eight, managed to hold a black belt in judo.

"So all in all," said Farber in a spasm of self-delight, "a typical *shikse* dilettante."

Beyond such ironies, I proceeded to undertake a short history of my father: How he had led a rough existence in Texas, Oklahoma and Kansas as a wrangler; how he had competed in rodeos, once even beating out Hoot Gibson for top bulldogging honors; how he had drifted into western movies—an extra at Fox, a stunt-man at Monogram, one of the featured "heavies" at Universal; how during this time he had designed and patented certain trick holsters with spring lock mechanisms to facilitate "fast draws."

And though I sought to set forth the singular saga of my father's later years—his progress from autodidact to Joycean scholar of the first rank—Farber would not hear me out; what fascinated him all along, I think, was my evident pride in my parents, the fact that they could afford me pleasure, that I enjoyed, actually enjoyed, their company. Thus, when I made mention of presenting my father with a horse to celebrate publication of his *Joyce and Yeats: Two Forms of Exile,* Farber pinched my both cheeks, squeezed my nose, plucked my beard and after a fit of coarse and ribald laughter said, *"Ah leyben uff der kepeleh!"* (Long life to your little head); when, further, I cited the spontaneous rides my father and I would take together, rides which might last as long as four and five days, Farber, crying "Wowee!" sloshed me with saliva.

He said, "Pals of the saddle!"

And he went on to say, "By you this is typical?"

"By me," I answered grandly, "this is typical."

"And maybe the two of you go . . . I can't think of the word . . . I heard it, oh, years and years ago in Sheepshead Bay. . . . It's with a boat, it's without a boat . . . FISHING!"

"Yes, we fished. And," I added, "on occasion . . . hunted."

We repeated the "By you this is typical?" "By me this is typical" routine, after which he called me *"nahrisher kind"* (foolish or unworldly child). And he set about giving me a picture, virtually a lithograph, of the relationship he and his father enjoyed. Nor was he speaking only for himself; on this he insisted. Generations, myriads, hosts, legions of Jewish boys, *ses frères, ses semblables,* seemed to be lined up in sized place lamenting and begging their runty fathers. . . .

"For what? Do I know? You take my pop—and he had partners who took him for plenty. Who needed we should be companions by the hunt? He wasn't Killdeer? So he was Killjoy. He wasn't Spencer Tracy? So I wasn't Mickey Rooney. Did I care? I didn't care. He batted me no balls,

I shagged him no flies. We didn't go off on safaris? All right, twice a year he'd *schlepp* me to the Lower East Side for two dented cans of Gillette Foamy discards and an unlabeled half-gallon of after-shave lotion you could use to pickle herrings. And on *Simchas Torah* we'd share a Chiclet together in his den, he had himself a lovely den, my mom had fixed up a special shelf in the linen closet and there he'd give out, he'd lay on me his special wisdom: 'Kiddo, sonny, don't be fooled like I was fooled for half my life. Because they'll try, oh how they'll try to and work hard and from all sides they'll want to put it over on you. Only hear me, believe: Let them charge a dime, let them charge a dollar, let them grind it fine and let them grind it coarse— but sonny, kiddo, all . . . talcum powder . . . is The Same!' But the thing is—this is the thing—he gave me what all Jewish fathers give all Jewish kids. A foul and sinister affliction which has no name. If it had a name, though, that name would be the Hoo-Hah syndrome.

"To know from the Hoo-Hah syndrome—and you shouldn't know from it—you have to let the calendar leaves exfoliate. Oh miserable little rat, you're eleven years old on sweet Saturday afternoon and you're home from the movies where you've seen . . . you've seen the Tailspin Tommy chapter. Or *Ceiling Zero*. Or *Men With Wings*. Planes are on your mind, only planes: two-winged Spads and China Clippers and slinky Stukas and stately Webley-Vickers. And your spirit is going ah, ah, ah, it's expanding like a gas. With fraternity. With loving-kindness. With sweet reason and innocent pleasure. Because in S. S. Kresge's for twenty-three cents you got . . .

" 'Hey, sonny, kiddo, what did you get?'

" 'A model airplane kit, Pop.'

" 'Hoo-Hah!'

" 'For the Cessna C-34, Pop.'

" 'Hoo-Hah!'

" 'Listen how you make it, Pop. Pop, you make it with

balsa wood and you make it with a very fine paper and a certain glue, airplane glue, and the motor—you know how you make the motor? With rubber bands!'

" 'Hoo-Hah . . . Hoo-Hah . . . Hoo-Hah. . . .' "

In the years that followed, avowed Farber, he was to hear this morbid, mocking "Hoo-Hah" when he offered to open a jar, to change a fuse, to drive a nail, to turn a screw, to press down a thumbtack, to free what was stuck, to oil what was squeaking, to plug or unplug, to install or remove, to paint or strip a surface, to shut off or turn on. And a terrible ineptitude was born; let him unto this day so much as look at a hammer and the hammer would shake its head and bleat, apologetically, "I'm not for a Jewish boy." Why, it would be easier for the Pope to change his religion than for him to change a tire. Was it his fault? It was not his fault nor even his father's fault. For even in the Old Testament the essential *klutziness* of his race stood inscribed. . . .

"You know why we had to leave Egypt in such a hurry? I'll tell you why: We were just finishing up the pyramids and one of us yells, 'V*ey*, we forgot to put in windows!' "

Thinking upon it, I am delighted that I rejected my first impulse to play the pompous pedagogue—citing all the many-sided reasons for the Jew's historic alienation from hand- and land-work—or to offer some commonplace along the lines of, "All gentiles are not plumbers and all Jews are not prophets."

What I did was rise, divest myself of jacket and tie and in the best Yiddish intonation I could manage announce, "You know, you've been a real schmuck."

Then for the next two hours, heedless of his housekeeper's howls of "Hey, Jinsberg!" and "All power to the Palestine guerrillas!," unmoved by Farber's own copious curses (Sample: "You should be lecturing at Union Theological, you should get there a little stroke and you should be able to say only, 'I gave to UJA, I gave to UJA.' "), I had him stooping and squatting and sweating at my car. Where firmly, levelly, in a tone that was both affable and angry, forceful and fawning, dealing with Farber as I might deal with a child, I compelled and cajoled him to have a go at changing a tire; this done—and he was meanwhile cackling and crowing like some great demented bird—I located for him points, plugs, condenser, vacuum advance, PC valve, crankcase, dipstick, voltage regulator and manifold. "Now, at once," I said, disassembling the carburetor air cleaner, "take hold of the automatic choke, then the linkage. Linkage . . . !" and he followed me along as I demonstrated basic procedures for dealing with a flooded engine. Presently he was addressing himself in the third person, like an Elizabethan tragic hero, crooning, "Farber, Farber, master craftsman, golden hands," promising me a two-year exemption from all scheduled ritual murders, also the right to squeeze rolls in any Jewish bakery of my choice.

I cannot report with certainty exactly when Farber bade me stay to dinner, though if I were compelled to pick the moment I would imagine it was after he had actually touched a set of points and I observed him quelling tears of happiness. No matter: Two cultures were to come together, two natures would alter and affect one another—indeed, so subtly yet so weightily that when his housekeeper came along with a demand for three million dollars in reparations to start a fund for those of her people killed while cleaning Flatbush windows I told her, quite uncharacteristically, that she would be best off completing her term paper on remedial looting.

Let time pass.

A month, six weeks.

In the name of research, or so I believe, I am spending a sample day with Farber, heading to some shopping-town fair. He is on this day "with it," he is "turned on," he is out to prey on the Real America. Yet his color is poor, his breath is noisy and congested, and I discern in his behavior strains of savagery and darkness and headlong despair. He tells me his wife, Marlene, is losing her marbles along with her period. Nine, ten times a day she calls him. From public places only. From the most crowded beauty parlors and boutique fitting rooms. From parties where old friends listened in on the extensions. While she denounced him retroactively. For throwing out, twelve years ago, her cultural anthropology notes. For letting her get slipcovers. For not letting her get slipcovers. For the failure of the Russian Revolution, the decline of the West, the phases of the moon. . . .

Meanwhile he hunches over the wheel of his car, driving like some murderous jockey. He beeps out on the horn "Hatikvah" and "Hava Nagila," he sticks his face out the window like a weapon, like a pervert exposing himself, and into the traffic stream yowls—why, what does he not yowl? —"Pigs should geld you!" . . . "Hose down m' T-shirt, Marthy, the minister's comin' tuh dinner" . . . "They're hirin' at GE" . . . "Warning—I brake for goyim!" Worse, far worse is his gift, his instinct for blundering; once blundered, he goes gleefully by four service stations back to back, ten cabbies imploring in unison, "Mac, need help, Mac?," a letter carrier twenty years on the same route, turns into some dreary development and cruises till he tracks down his game: a pinched, goggle-eyed, tennis-white woman holding private conversations with herself about the State Department and the Supreme Court, shaking a palsied fist at a neighbor's psychedelic Volkswagen. "Miss, hoo-hoo sveetie"—he is shaking open a huge city map—"You gots maybe hah second?" And while she turns upon him a loony primal creature look, the look of a dog setting itself to chase a car, he solicits directions from her in Talmudic singsong, at the end kissing her hands and offering boxes of Passover matzos at substantial discount.

Then off again.

By the longest route, the worst road.

I breathe heaving pre-vomity gulps, I hear myself moaning. I cry, "Mercy!," then "*Rachmoniss*!"

I ask myself, "This is me?"

And the answer is returned, "It's you, it's you!"

As stopped at a crosswalk I link my voice to Farber's voice in a flutely wail of "One, two, three, four/ Who won the Six-Day War?"

As Farber teaches me the *krechtz*—that ponderous trochee issued from the depths of the diaphragm and signifying, all at once, the sorrows of Job, the indecision of Hamlet, Jeremiah-like comment on man's fate.

He mimics and mocks me till I achieve some small mastery of the critical Yiddish pronunciations, till my *nyoo* evolves into *new*, then *nu*; my *hoots-par* into *hutzpah*; my *holly* into *chollee*.

By rote and without respite, by means of heady praise and barbarous abuse, he trains me to tell Jewish jokes. I am at first fearful and faltering, my voice rises and falls in just the wrong places, chokes on phlegm and guilt. After all, I warn myself, this is why, precisely why, they have an Anti-Defamation League. Then with God's help it comes, it simply comes, and I am suddenly speaking as though through a dybbuk: *Ginsberg meets Lefkowitz why you so depressed and the herring looks up and the herring says if I didn't see him put on the medicine I should choke on the first bite only I don't have linings.*

I am afflicted with anomie, acedia, wanhope—*meshugass,* states my notes, and the word is three times underscored— as Farber has me belt out lewd, lachrymose Yiddish ballads, as we pull into the shopping-town plaza and he, then I, then both together—

No matter.

None, happily none hear us.

For at that moment two clowns come at us with cowbells.

"I love their church socials," says Farber, instantly improvising something about raffling off a goiter. And while I murmur a wistful *"Ave atque vale"* to my tenure, my forthcoming sabbatical, my seat on the academic senate, he engages a young housewife, praising her skin for its liver spots and stretch marks, plucking from her nerveless fingers a copy of *Woman's Day*. " 'Little did I suspect,' " he pretends to read, " 'the divine pleasures that awaited my love hole when first I beheld that massive blood-gorged organ. Squeezing my clit, I begged him with all my heart to fill me full of it. . . .' "

He is still gripping the *Woman's Day* when I heave and hustle him into the thick of the crowd toward the Kitty Kelly, where forty watts of loudspeaker drown him out with their yockering. . . .

"Say, Mary, do you remember when they first broke ground for our San Isidro Shopping-Town?"

"Yes, Tom, and now it's celebrating A DECADE OF COMMUNITY SERVICE."

"With rides for the kiddies and sales galore in every store."

"And Mommy, Mommy, don't forget the prizes!"

"You're right, Billy. We're all eligible for those GRAND PRIZES—and there's no purchase necessary."

"Say, Mary, do you remember when they first broke ground for our—"

In time I will undoubtedly sort out my emotions, put a name to my state of mind. Did I suffer a spasm of *folie à deux*? Or was I subsumed, ingested—enFarbered?

For I know only that while we head toward the heart of the fair I am receiving sensations as though through Farber's skin, Farber's nerves, I am walking—

How am I walking?

With tiny twirling steps.

With a shuffle, a stoop.

Clutching invisible carpetbags.

"*Goyim,*" I very nearly cry, gazing, glaring at orange drink the color of healthy urine. At khaki pizza wedges. At boiled franks and scabrous mustard jars. At spastic marionettes on wires that could hold up bridges. At runny-colored pennants barely able to flutter. At the kiddy roller coaster on rusty tracks. At a donkey engine shimmering off its white kerosene stink.

And still I step—say, rather, I *schlepp*—along with Farber. Good, good, I silently exclaim, give it to them . . . Them!

Smite them, *schmeiss* them! And by a kind of telepathic concentration I direct him as though he were a golem to an orange-headed lady collecting monies for a volunteer ambulance. "By you this is fund raising?" he bawls into her hearing aid. "Darling, fund raising is not for you people. It's not your bag. In fact bags aren't even your bag because you know who controls the whole pocketbook trade. All right, we can't build your septic tanks, you can't raise our funds."

Then in a piercing falsetto: "We have trespassed, we have been faithless, we have robbed, we have wrought unrighteousness, we have hardened our hearts and tenderized our meats, we have joined book clubs, we have mocked Ed Sullivan, we have entered the *Reader's Digest* Grand Sweepstakes, we have advertised in the *Pennysaver*, we have finished our basements, we have put antique bottles in our windows, we have taken old milk cans and converted them into umbrella stands, we have made a sacrament of the cookout. . . ."

But in the middle of things (he is caroling "Plehnt hah tree in Eretz Yisroel for Norman Vincent Peale") two shopping carts collide and a can of Ajax bursts at Farber's feet.

Upon this can he fixes a look—how shall I write of this look? Likening it to what? To Hector reading his fate in the eyes of Achilles? To a vampire beholding the cross? To King Kong before he takes his long tumble down the Empire State Building? To Laurel, cringing as he awaits the punishments of Hardy?

His eye is still on the Ajax, his stance catatonic, as a woman wearing a smoky gold pants suit and a sleepily sensual smile diminishes her mouth and jangles her bracelets at him.

"If," she says, "if you are Jules Farber, you once had my brother for a landlord."

Though I have five-and-a-half single-spaced pages of notes on her (*face painted into the lidless thin-lipped mask of an oriental despot . . . Fu Manchu fingernails . . . ferocious over-articulation*) I will report, perhaps out of deference to the human relations agencies, only her last five minutes or so of monologue, starting as she is folding away a walletful of snapshots taking "her Jeffrey" from potty to playschool to the moment when he is winding a set of phylacteries around the wrong arm.

". . . Julie, darling, if we ever did a smart thing and if we ever did a wise thing it was to come here and leave behind the narrow restrictions of our ghettoized environment. Right now if you asked me, 'Where are your roots?' I would answer, 'You wish to know where our roots are? Our roots are here, here we have made our roots.' This decision, when we decided to put our roots down here was the wisest thing we could have done because our kids love it. They grow up and are raised with nature, they live what is known as A MORE NATURAL LIFE. My Sandy tells me all the time, I am referring to my eighteen-year-old daughter, people don't believe me that I have an eighteen-year-old daughter, 'Mom, I am ever so glad we became enrooted here as I now feel part of a pluralistic society.' And the remarkable thing is that since we came here we are much more interested in things of Judaic nature; until recently I didn't know what an *Oneg Shabbat* was. Also I had a stereotyped idea of what your typical rabbi was. On account of here we have a Dr. Brian, his name is Dr. Brian Shapiro but he enjoys being called Dr. Brian or Dr. Rack and Pinion because he goes in for sports cars—and this is a youthful chap with presence; he looks like Steve McQueen and he talks like Walter Pidgeon. And you never have to be afraid of rapping with him on a topic of nonsectarian importance. If you say to him, 'Dr. Brian, what should I do that my husband is discussing with me about indulging in group sex?' he is straight, he is open and absolutely forthright. Right away he tells you, 'Seek the advice and professional guidance of an expert counselor.' This is typical of our outstanding Jewish leadership, this is why we are secure and accepted and enrooted here. To the extent, Julie darling, that they have for us a special Jewish seat on the Town Council. That they run in cable TV so we should be able to watch our 'Eternal Light.' That their Grand Union took in lately the entire Manischewitz soup line. We're accepted, we're homogeneous, Julie darling; they buy their watch bands from us, we buy our Diesel fuel from them. . . ."

Around this time he kisses her. In the center of her pancaked brow, on the corners of her Vaselined mouth. It is the kiss a boy might bestow upon his mother in a cancer ward, the kiss some remote ancestor comes to seek in dreams.

And as we enter the discount house I am declaiming, "*I must confess we come not to be kings: That's not our fault.*" And Farber is wishing upon me an old age in a substandard nursing home. Where in the name of occupational therapy I will end my days flicking chickens.

I was at various times privileged to hear Farber's views on womankind in general and the gentile woman in particular, and what follows is a verbatim transcript of these views recorded when Farber, simultaneously at the peak of his power and the end of his rope, managed to fuse vision and style with, I believe, unsurpassed intensity. And since the immediate occasion for his outburst was a visit from his wife, Marlene, I am compelled, however unhappily, to outline what passed between them.

She had come on this day to deliver, in accordance with the terms of their separation agreement, the *bondit* (clever little rogue or rascal; so Farber, absolutely devoid of irony, calls Mitchell, their autistic five-year-old) for an obligatory weekend at Malibu. Before too long Farber has flung her to the floor and emptied around and upon her the contents of Mitchell's little suitcase. "Slob! Cow! Stepmother! What"— he hurls something at her like a harpoon—"what did you do to his toothbrush! What? You dipped it first in shit?" Next he holds up three socks and announces that all three are mismatched. He points out further that this "packer of packers" who has omitted rainwear, thermometer, vitamins, nonallergenic soap and undershirts has thrown in—"You know what she throws in?" He counts out one, two, three, four abused facial tissues. Which he pushes into her face, crying, "*Shikse* bitch, how many Jews did your father kill? 'Ja, ja, I vuss durink der Hitler time vurking for Jenny Grossinger in der Brazil chungles; I vass overseer for onion roll farm. . . .' "

Fifteen minutes later Marlene has fled, wordlessly weeping and holding together her panties, savaged by Farber in a search for the cross he swears she keeps at all times about her person. We have moved to the beach, where I slice a two-pound Isaac Gellis salami with my Swiss Guard pocket-knife. Mitchell is picking off his face a sizable scab and packing the resultant aperture with a poultice made from spittle and sand as Farber, after giving him compulsive love-bites, after licking at his ears, his navel, starts to speak. Like Lear in the storm, like Ahab on the bridge.

"In my life I had . . . what? Maybe three big shocks. Shock number one was when I heard Cary Grant was Jewish. Shock number two was finding out how Jell-O, pure, pathetic, parveh Jell-O, sweet ecumenical Jell-O what you could eat with milk *or* meat—Jell-O was not kosher. But you know what was? Drake's Devil Dogs! To eat them you had to look like—you know who you had to look like? Wayne Morris.

"Notice, you'll notice I'm forgetting small stuff and tiny traumas. Roosevelt wouldn't trade trucks for Jews? All right, it wasn't nice, it wasn't the way a *mensch* should act. Still— still I understood; to a *goy* a truck means a lot. Then you figure . . . *his* people were exploring, *his* people were discovering, *his* people were opening up. While your people— your people were looking and looking for a nice four-room apartment, the rooms had to be off the foyer. It didn't hurt? It hurt, it hurt. But where did it compare to shock number three?

"To understand shock number three you'd have to be in the car with my Mom and Dad heading along Ocean Avenue for a little seafood at Lundy's. It's 1947, Flatbush's Age of Gold. The *schvartzers* are still a double fare away and doing windows at thirty-five cents a window. Where you look is a Barton's and Ebinger's, by appointment official bakers to the Brooklyn Irish, is featuring *chalah* on Friday. Bubbees, ancient bubbees who should be in antique satin and lavalieres, are wearing toreador pants and wedgies. Big *zoftig* young mothers push their English prams and you can hear them practically calling each to each, 'We have it so nice' . . . 'We have it so fine' . . . 'We have it so good.' One of whose daughters—I'm seventeen years old but my young Jewish life is already out like a good canasta hand—I will marry. A good strong thumper of a Brooklyn Girl, a Brownsville Beckie training me and taming me to slipcovers and scouring powder and bungalow colony summers; while I got diabetes she's got diamonds. Who wanted better, who knew better . . . ?

"Until my Pop starts in.

" 'Kiddo, marry only Jewish girls and hire only *shikses*.'

"Why?

" 'Because the Jewish working girl,' he tells me, 'does not like to work.'

"See, he has a Sharon Goldstein . . . !

" 'I clocked her once in the bathroom, kiddo, it came to thirty-eight minutes. So I knocked on the door, I told her stay and make an even forty.'

"Six months she worked for him, and in those six months . . .

" 'She didn't change her typewriter ribbon or her piece of carbon paper. If God called she'd get His name wrong. Rush orders she files under Pending but luncheonette menus go into Immediate Attention.'

"But he had once a Carolee Falvey. . . .

" 'A workhorse, kiddo, a wonder girl. Who saved every penny, every nickel. Who grudged herself even a copy of the *Catholic Tablet*. Why? To help out the hubby. That's what she called him: The . . . Hubby.'

"And my mother picks up the beat.

" 'I do not like to knock my own, but between you and

I and the lamppost, it must absolutely go no further, I would love to know the secret, do they learn it in their churches, that if you look at the average commonplace little *shikse* you see a true-blue wife who doesn't have on her mind only minks and chinks. In our building you see a Myrtle Burke, she dresses in *shikse shmattahs*, she camps out with her Floyd in Lake George where they rent you out a whole island for fifteen dollars a week, she has a permanent maybe once a year on her Easter and she scrapes her own floors. Every morning I meet her at the incinerator, I ask her, "Myrtle, what smells so deliciously from your house?" "Oh, I am just whipping up"—whipping up, you hear—"a batch of hot biscuits is all." Three nights she's a hostess for Schrafft's, two days she makes extension cords and every other weekend she's a relief girl at Woolworth. *She* you don't see trying on and taking off at Ohrbach's. From *her* you wouldn't get notes, *Honey*, if I'm late from the theater take the clothes from the dryer and the cold cuts from the refrigerator.'

"Seriously, this is serious, if you're looking for logic don't look for logic. Because on the one hand my mom would come back from Sisterhood luncheons with a napkinful of butter cookies and a headful of statistics on mixed marriage, the perils and pitfalls of. On the other hand she would call the dentist for a cleaning and I'd hear, 'Doctor, if you don't mind, I have nothing against Sadie, Sadie is a good soul and it's not her fault if she talks a little too much, I am sure the majority of your patients enjoy hearing the courses she's taking at the New School for Social Research, but for my gingivitis I am better off with May Brown, I like May Brown's gum work and also her loyalty to you, she doesn't complain that she has to come in *Simchas Torah*.'

"Or every Monday and Thursday she'd collect for a different disease and every Monday and Thursday it was, 'Nine thousand dollars for hiatus hernia, Mrs. Levine, is a personal insult, after all, you spent more for your daughter's linen shower, at least put to it another thousand, I am ashamed to write you down for less than ten thousand, make believe you gave the daughter a few more Fieldcrest towels.'

"Ah, but when she rang her nonsectarian doorbells— 'That's Mrs. Riley with an E, right, am I right? Here is the triplicate receipt for your six cents, naturally a letter from the president of our drive will shortly be forthcoming, but let me meanwhile say personally that those two deposit bottles will go a long way toward providing a crucially needed research center, would you mind if we named after you a pavilion . . . ?'

"And my pop—my pop who knew every last little Jewish atrocity—my pop who could give you the name of the first Jew to get a low back pain—my pop who claimed that a Jewish fortune-teller warned Davy Crockett to stay away from the Alamo—go, go believe this very same UJA Man of the Year would absolutely not eat his lunch till three o'clock in the afternoon because that's when Maggie came on duty. 'With Maggie I got not a waitress but a caterer, kiddo, this *shikse* is accommodating, she's what you call an accommodating *shikse*, a Jewish waitress would also do what she does, sure, a Jewish waitress right away brings you such icy ice water.'

"Put him in a Jewish hospital and on a bed which he, he himself contributed, then let Nurse Horowitz bend over this bed to spoon-feed him and he looks at her with a George Sanders leer, he twists his mouth with a George Sanders twist . . . 'Ah-ha, yes, m'dear, to be sure, keep jiggling the bed more, very good, I'll be so in pain, m'dear, I'll maybe forget to report how certain parties are snappy when requested for a little double crostic help.' Yeah yeah, but when Nurse Bateshaw makes love to the glazed fruits from his thirty-dollar steamer basket it's 'Help yourself, Sister of Mercy, selfless person, finish up the marzipan and don't worry as there will be awaiting you a lovely little gratuity, what you did for me Florence Nightingale wouldn't do, in my life I never had a pillow patted the way you patted it, our common mutual God should only bless you for your ministrations. . . .'

"Am I blaming them? I'm not blaming them. Look, from all sides, from the top and bottom of my culture they were lined up to lay it on me. My fate, my destiny was in the hands of—not Moses Maimonides, but Louis B. Mayer. With his Anne Rutherfords and June Preissers and Greer Garsons. I don't say he should have had them talking like Myron Cohen or spreading newspaper on the floor or diving into pickle barrels or dripping chicken blood. But once, only once show them watching a scale, yelling from a window, grating a little horseradish. You want to make *Quo Vadis?* and *Ben Hur?* Go ahead, you're entitled. Give a little boost, though, to your own. It's costing you anyway for a nativity scene, so punch up the Virgin Mary part. 'Cheapskates, lice, pascudnyakim! You see my presents? Frankincense, myrrh . . . I need it badly. I still got in my closet a jar garlic powder, it's not touched because by me spices are poison. Not even a box bridge mix, in Galilee they're selling the best bridge mix fifty-nine shekels a pound. Do I care? I'm only embarrassed for the innkeeper. . . .' "

(Farber's attention was diverted at this time by Mitchell, who had removed his trunks and urinated into a stiff wind. For the next twelve or fifteen minutes he was engaged in toweling "the *bondit*" and starting him off on a Flintstones Paste and Stick kit. Given these circumstances, I have elected to omit Farber's unstructured speculations about the absence of a true Jewish pornography—i.e., "First I'll finish cleaning between the burners, then you can sixty-nine me stiff!"— and move directly to the next stage of his thought. It should be kept in mind that the material which now follows deals with Farber's attendance at Erasmus Hall High School, located in the geographical and cultural center of Flatbush.)

"Believe me, Erasmus produced plenty of Jewish pussy. Political pussy, ready to fuck and suck for a Howard Fast book. Avant-garde pussy—for a kind word and a copper bracelet they'd climb the twenty flights to a cold-water flat.

Good, giving pussy; from them you could get library cards and class notes and dutch treat dates and a pathetic little hand-job on the roof. Red-hot Zionist pussy: On a forty-mile hike you could stinkfinger them and still they wouldn't break stride.

"In fact there was one—Joanie Ziefler—when she went down the corridors you'd hear 'Wowwowee, I'd like to fuck that! That, yuh, that I'd like to fuck!' And these were the teachers. White on white teeth . . . tits like knapsacks . . . one of those tremendous Manhattan Beach tans. Sensitive, yet, and refined. She *dahnced*, she wrote not just poems but sonnet sequences, she carried around two copies of *The Prophet* and she was building a collection of pre-Columbian art. For this little *pishikeh* you didn't need to worry; the worst that would happen to her was she'd take taxis to Mexico City, she'd spend summers with Australian Bushmen, she'd direct documentaries, she'd open a coffee house, she'd own four seal point Siamese cats named Eros, Thanatos, Megaton and Overkill.

"And who—who did Joanie openly covet?

"After whom do you think she hankered and hungered?

"Ah, but you had an interest in her? That's how I was interested!

"No.

"No no!

"Give me better Darlene Brown. And Gladys Parmelee. And Elsa Kawa.

"They would be in Dubrow's Cafeteria at the *shikse* table talking Pitman and Gregg and 'I'm gettin' a sixty in Business English' and 'My sister Francine is tryin' to decide between the veil and the phone company' and 'Remember the medallion my Old Lady gave me? It was blessed by the Holy Fodder? I lost it in Riis Pork.'

"With them—Them!—you should have heard me!

" 'Say, I wonder if by chance you girls had occasion to look at the October 18th *New Republic*. Because you would definitely have been interested in the tough-minded thrust of

Irving Howe's realpolitik.' I'd follow them home, on the way buying them Carvel Custard banana boats, talking Marx and Lenin. I'd invite them to oboe recitals at Carnegie Hall, film festivals at the Museum of Modern Art, readings at the Joyce Society.

"Oh, oh the respect I gave them!

"They could have tattoos, they could smell from Lysol and lard, they could have complexions the color of evaporated milk. . . .

"But between those dehydrated legs I believed—

"Listen what I believed!

"*Shikses . . . were . . . different.*

"Where different? How different?

"*Different!*

"Jewish girls had big black things there. Named, properly and with absolute accuracy . . . *Cunts! Boxes! Twats! Snatches!* Shaggy, hairy dust-collectors. Swatches of wall-to-wall carpeting! Pads of Brillo! Organs like gorgons!

"But *shikses*—hidden under their communion white panties were those soft and downy teeny-tinys. A golden fleece. A cunnie, a bunnie, a quim, a kumquat, a joy-toy, a honey pot. The tip of a tress could cover them or a very small fig leaf. Trouble-free, warranted for parts and labor. Granted, given, these divinities, these marvelous maidens got, oh once a month they got—oh, not these massive, these copious Jewish menstruations where the world has to come to an end: 'You'll call them, you'll thank them, you'll have them mail you the Nobel Prize because right now for your wife a trip to Sweden is out.' But *shikses?* Give them half a Midol tablet and they'll break wild horses, they'll surf-cast, they'll go down waterfalls, they'll skin-dive. . . ."

A minute later Farber, with my assistance, was compelled to pry Mitchell's jaws apart in an effort to make him disgorge the remains of two, perhaps three crayons. And while we were both badly bitten I suspect I sustained somewhat more damage than Farber. For apart from the fact that my desert boots—unfortunately fawn-colored—were so vomit-stained that I immediately discarded them, the *bondit* managed to draw blood from the heel of my right palm; the depth and mixed dirt of the laceration required suturing and an antitetanus booster. Withal, he would seem to have taken a liking to me, and at Farber's insistence I walked him up and down and back and forth along the beach, for long stretches mounting him on my back and galloping into the surf while he beat me about the region of my mastoids and Farber, running behind, lashed my buttocks with a wet towel.

In this fashion we were compelled to cover, by my rough reckoning, upwards of a mile till the *bondit* was gentled. During our trek back Farber resumed his discourse; lacking at the time either notebook or cassette I must rely upon memory in claiming that till his marriage Farber regarded the *shikse* as the ultimate in both sex and servitude, as a docile dummy, a selfless succubus trained to perform unnatural acts while installing copper plumbing and 220-volt wiring. To please her Jewish boy—for dumb as she was she knew what was good—she set about pleasing his mother. Who, after the first pangs and pains, would boast of her before cousins' clubs: "You ought to see how we're chums, she calls me Mother Goldie, from her Mother Goldie she wants to learn all our Jewish things, you should see how she keeps me on my toes, if I go to the toilet on *Shabbos* she runs after, 'Mother Goldie, don't be tearin' no toilet paper.'"

But then, en route to New York City after emceeing a Swinging Singles Weekend at Fendabenda Lodge in Ellenville, the *Moloch Hamoviss*—Hebrew for the Angel of Death—sent him his Marlene. Via Mohawk Airlines, where she was employed as a stewardess. Symbolically, her first direct words to Farber were "That will be a dollar, sir." For in no time everything was in her name; even, he swore, his name was in her name. Let her uncap a tube of vaginal jelly and she had him signing fifty thousand dollar annuities. Though she went about mumbling "Salt white, pepper black, mustard green, ketchup red," though she had twice lighted an oven—and one of those times represented a suicide attempt—she was never done renovating the kitchen. Five days before and three days after the curse was upon her she would be so powerfully stirred against Farber that she used to trap his hand between her hands and pinch out the little hairs from around his wrist. Unto the follicles. When his parents came bearing Patek Philippe watches, Baccarat crystal, the keys to a helicopter, the deed to two acres in downtown Dallas, the 1967 receipts for the IRT's 34th Street station, she made pointed complaint about her lack of drawer space. Give her, though, an empty carton from her father and she would be rubbing at it all day: "It's a Nabisco, a 1949 corrugated Nabisco, you never see these anymore, 1949 was a vintage year for Nabisco. . . ."

Still he believed, he persisted in believing that from the mingling of bloods—her people had poured salt upon cities, his upon chickens—from the mating of 4-H queen and three-sewer hitter they would beget stationwagonsful of leggy freckled Baal-Shem-Tovs capable of pitching horseshoes and exorcising demons, equally at home in firehouse and discount house.

And in point of fact the *bondit*, like many another autistic child, had as infant and toddler been a superbly endowed specimen. "A blondie, a buster, a butterball," claimed Farber when we reached our blanket and resumed taping.

"Ponies would whinny after him, he should only be photographed on their backs.

"To sneak a peek at him gypsies took turns being abandoned on our doorstep.

"Yeshivahs donated brand-new clothes for him. . . . Pigeons saved him their best crumbs.

"A couple would come for dinner and when the wife saw him she'd open a mouth on her husband, 'Let's go, dummy, it's the middle of the month, moron. . . .' In the elevator she'd start doing natural childbirth exercises."

(At this juncture Farber grabs the *bondit* who giggles in shrieking peals and they wrestle each other to the ground.

Miming violent struggle, then panic, then powerlessness, Farber permits himself to be pinned. Very severely he trumpets into the *bondit*'s face, "Daddy doesn't like you!" To which the *bondit* makes reply—and I have played this section of tape several times to ascertain the precise syllabification—"Droodle, garoonish, hasplesh." Whereupon Farber flips him gently over his back, presses and grinds him into his belly and croons, "Daddy doesn't like you, ah, ah, ah, no, oh no, nah, Daddy LOVES you . . . !" I taped perhaps three minutes more, during which time Farber begged and begged the *bondit* to point, only to point, at various parts of the body; when his tenth call for "Nosey" was unavailing I turned away my microphone and filled the balance of the reel with sea sound.)

April 17, 1973
Written in haste because I have to start
putting away my Passover dishes

Dear Chandler:
  Why not?
  You absolutely have all permission on the enclosed signed form to make full utilization of any or all parts of the tapes made during my visit to my late brother. I can say only "Thank God" that no more than my voice and words spoken by same will show up as I wouldn't want America to know Jules had himself such a fatty for a sister; the individual who now resembles a young truck horse once upon a time got into a junior eleven.
  Grief-stricken though I still am I and my many friends continue to derive many a laugh from my tale of that delightful afternoon and how I mistook you for being Jewish. Believe me, you don't look Jewish, but you gave a very Jewish impression, and when you referred to the taste of that sponge cake as being "very geshmock" and also mentioned to Julie that the "schvartzer" was late that morning I was convinced.

Let me know what more help I can provide to keep my brother's memory and work evergreen. And I need not tell you, Chandler, that should you find yourself in the near future—look, you never know—by the Park Slope section of Brooklyn you must make it your business to come say "hello." Call beforehand to make sure, and if you get no answer keep on trying as I am in and out working to fulfill my manifold responsibilities for the Young Israel Organization.

Warmest wishes, fondest personal regards,
Mrs. Lillian Federman

P.S. I still think you give a Jewish impression.

". . . You know from when I've been on the go? Since . . . early . . . morning. Even in California your sister had to make a condolence call. You remember Pop's Cousin Shura Lipsky? Ooh, you should remember! The very good-natured little woman with the crazy eyes, they were from a glandular condition. She had the corner store on Coney Island Avenue near Kings Highway, she carried only nuts. What happened I forgot, either she broke a hip or chipped herself in the pelvis and she won a big negligence suit against Davega and she came out here years ago to live with her son Herbie who had a taxi service; he would take people from the candy store to the subway for a dime a person. I hate to tell you what they charge now. You know what they're charging? Seventy-five cents! Anyway, Shura's father-in-law died. I will say about him what Shura said: 'He was . . . some . . . man!' Believe me, very few fathers-in-law love their daughters-in-law the way he loved her; show me another father-in-law who'll come lay linoleum for his daughter-in-law on a day that busted all heat records for twenty-three years. I remember my Hershey's camp trunk arrived that day and I said to the truckman, 'You know something? Today is going to be . . . a real scorcher!' And when was it? Naturally! *Erev* Yom Kippur. Ooh, no! No, no! Chandler, you're thinking of Passover. Don't worry about it, my feelings are not hurt and I also make similar mistakes. Till I saw on TV *The King of Kings* I never knew there was a difference between Mary Magdalene and Virgin Mary. . . ."

(*Farber's housekeeper arrives,* my notes show. While she slams about, Farber lets her know that she has kept the faith, that in all their time together she has never failed him on a Thursday, this being her day to bust the Disposal. Mrs. Federman remarks over her brother's great good luck, calls jokingly into the kitchen to inquire whether Beulah could sometimes give her a day. On alternate Wednesdays. She fails to hear or chooses not to hear Beulah's "Eat plaster!")

". . . I see you're writing notes, Chandler, as long as you're writing put down a reminder that the minute I leave here I should go to the Japanese Barn because I promised Aunt Pearlie a certain set of pots. These are pots they once had in A&S but somehow you don't see them anymore. In fact I had an argument with the A&S buyer; months and months and months he's promising me the pots are coming: They're coming, oh they're coming, that's all I heard from him. Finally I went over his head in a nice way to ask the assistant manager when he expects the shipment and the man fell on me . . . ooh! He was very lucky I was parked illegally and had already two tickets that month. The first one I really didn't deserve, it was a technicality. I happened to be *technically* by the loading zone in front of Waldbaum's and a policeman came over. 'Hey, lady, you're by the loading zone.' So I told him, 'Officer, I know I should not *technically* park here, only I'm going into the store for two seconds on what you could call an errand of mercy for a neighbor who had her both breasts removed, I don't have to tell you, officer, what a terrible operation this is, we shouldn't know from it, she needs a *yahrzeit* lamp or memorial tumbler in honor of a close relation who is deceased, I even have the exact change, you'll see how I'll be in and out, one-two-three. . . .'

"What I should have done was to get on the six-or-less items line, the checkout girl would have definitely let me through even though it turned out I had a few extra items because I remembered my neighbor Rose—when I get back to the hotel I should call her and find out how she did on her pap test—Rose begged me to buy her six cans of the dietetic mixed fruits. That's my nature, Julie can tell you, in my building they call me 'Lillian the Bringer.' They ought to call me better 'Lillian the Lemon' because by rights I should have done favors for Rose the way she did them for me; I was five weeks in traction, she wouldn't even pick up my mail.

"Anyway, on one of the regular lines I see Zeena Sugarman from the Young Israel—she's the one who when we had that sex expert for a speaker raised her hand and asked if she might put to him a penetrating question—and I ask her, 'Zeena, may I please get ahead of you with just these few little items?' She was all set to let me into the line when a man—this is what's so unusual, a man usually doesn't have that pettiness—the man gives me an argument. 'What's the big idea!' and 'What are you, there, a special case?' I answered him, 'Sir, I really really don't think I wish to enter with you into a prolonged debate but you ought to drop dead and be slightly ashamed of yourself as I am helping out a neighbor who had her both breasts amputated. I would call you an animal except even an animal shows more human feeling, if a bunch of elephants see another elephant hurt they try at least to give him a hand with their trunks.' And meanwhile—meanwhile Zeena takes her pocketbook and . . . in the face. She whacks him some *zetz* in the face! Chandler, you know what a *zetz* is? I see, I see he knows, ooh, I'm going to watch myself with him. . . ."

(Trouble from the housekeeper, who rages over the absence of Brillo. "The Jews use all the Brillo." "She's not altogether wrong," Mrs. Federman says to us. "You're not altogether wrong," she says to the housekeeper, giving her from the kitchen door an affable analysis of the relationship between the laws of kashruth and the Jewish instinct "for immaculate cleanliness." Turning to us she announces, sotto voce, that the space between stove and refrigerator is in a state of monumental neglect. ("V,E,R,Y *shmutzy*.") Turning back to the housekeeper she says, "By the way, your James Baldwin is some fine little writer. If I call him 'Little,' " she adds, "I'm talking only his height; look, for his physical stature this is a nicely built man. . . .")

". . . You should by now realize two things about your sister. Number one is she can be in the middle of space and get a satellite in her eye, and number two is where she travels she can meet a familiar party. So while waiting for my luggage to come off the plane I go, 'Oh oh, it feels like something in my eye.' Right next to me is a man who says, 'Do not rub, rubbing is THE WORST THING to do.' I told him he should not worry, I am an old hand at getting things in my eye. He says, 'Don't think I am trying to pick you up, but I have a little something to perhaps irrigate away the embedded foreign object in your eye.' I answered him to the effect that if he was looking to pick up somebody I was positive he could do better than a fatty such as myself. So he lifts back my lid and from a little bottle squeezes in TWO DROPS which right away do the job. I tell him, 'You have a wonderful touch.' 'When it comes to foreign object removal,' he answers, 'I had a good teacher because my father was a druggist and he had to do foreign object removal ten and twelve times a day.'

"Why I don't know, but something told me to ask him if his father had the drugstore called Ethical Pharmacy near the New Lots Avenue Station of the IRT which gave you good buys on Revlon. No, it seems his father's store was in Columbus, Ohio. . . ."

(Byplay between Mrs. Federman and the housekeeper. Mrs. Federman: "Would it be troubling you if I asked for a glass of COLD WATER?" Housekeeper: "It would." Mrs. Federman: "You're just like I am, I during cleanup chores also hate interruption; I won't even put the radio on unless I know they're playing Diana Ross or Aretha Franklin records.")

". . . Take Mitchell*eh* back with me because you know what he'd have with me? He'd have A . . . Swell . . . Time. Why not? He could play again with Adam from across the street, I bet if you said to him, 'Mitchell*eh*, you remember Adam?' he'd positively remember. Because this is some little Adam. Smart—they don't come any smarter! I saw last year when he played with Mitchell*eh*, another kid would have hit and scratched back, not Adam, he came running across the street to me, 'Mrs. Federman, I think your nephew is A . . . Trifle . . . DISTURBED,' I couldn't get over that a kid would use such terminology, now he's taking guitar lessons, I get such a kick when I see him go for his lessons, the guitar is bigger than he is.

"Look, I think the whole trouble with Mitchell*eh* is— you know what it is? He's not autistic . . . and he's *not* brain-damaged . . . and he's *not* retarded. He's what you call AN . . . UNDERACHIEVER. In other words he is not doing, he is not achieving up to his optimum and full potential. And So . . . What! I'll say to you what Dr. Zogbaum said to my friend Irma; Irma was worried because her boy wasn't doing well in school and he told her, 'You know what? Get him a newspaper route!' And that newspaper route did for the boy—I'll tell you what it did. Wonders! He became highly independent and he became responsible and he became a real little *mensch*. All right, he had a freak accident: He's riding along and a milk bottle hits him from a fire escape. . . .

"Now let's say Mitchell*eh* is a little young for a newspaper route, but—maybe he could perform little chores. Maybe he could walk a dog for somebody. Or maybe he could feed their goldfish. Give him something, in other words, to bring out his common sense. This is what I did when he was with me. For example, I took him once to Waldbaum's, we shopped—you notice how I'm stressing

the 'we,' because I made it a regular cooperative enterprise
and joint venture; I would tell him, 'See, Mitchell*eh*, now,
now Mitchell*eh* we're buying Waldbaum's cream cheese,
now we're buying the bialys, we'll have . . . bialys and cream
cheese.' Then we went to the checkout counter, we're at the
checkout counter and I say, 'Maybe Mitchell*eh* would like
to take out the stuff from the shopping cart for Aunt Lily?'
And let me tell you—with the autism . . . and *with* the
retarding he showed a whole lot of common sense the way
he took out everything. First he took out and stacked the
cans, then he took out all the vegetables, then all the paper
products. In fact, Henrietta the checkout girl had to ask
me if this was the little nephew who is supposed to have
something wrong with him; she even gave him two hopjes.
H, O, P, J, E, S, Chandler. Your friend is cute, Julie. I see
he's embarrassed. Chandler, what are you embarrassed? Let
me tell you something. May I tell you something? In my
experience most of, the majority of gentile people make the
same mistake. Mention 'hopje' to a gentile person and he
thinks it's a Jewish word. Marlene also—this is when we
were . . . Very Close; people used to say they never saw
sisters-in-law get along so beautifully—when we went shopping in the appetizing stores she'd beg me, 'Lily, don't forget to buy the Jewish hopjes. . . .' "

(Mrs. Federman unlooses a *"Gevald!"* that must have
registered 8.2 on the Richter Scale. She remembers, it seems,
that her husband will be calling at the hotel and she must
remind him that this is the day for Waldbaum's early clos-
ing. While Farber and I work to repair and repack her two
torn Waldbaum's shopping bags she takes her leave of the
housekeeper: "This is your last chance, Beulah, Beulah, how
about flying back with me?" A "Go crash in the Negev"
floats placidly back.)

". . . Which reminds me that this summer, we should
only live and be well, I'm definitely taking off two weeks to
go to Israel; I'm the only one almost in my whole building

who hasn't been. Also no more kidding around, this time I check myself into the Mount Sinai weight reduction clinic. It'll be nice, I'll bring along my old Speedwriting book and I can finish finally Abba Eban's *My People*, I never got past the part where they expel us from Spain. Believe me, I'm a college graduate who was on the dean's list and my girl reads more than I read; in fact, I borrow her gothic mysteries. You think it doesn't depress me? It depresses me plenty. In the middle of the night it gives me . . . a grabbing. And I start thinking, ooh . . . such things. My happiest dream lately is I dream I'm dead. Is it change of life or is it our Indochina policy? Not that I know what's happening there, I'm so behind in the newspapers. My friend Norma Rappaport came once to the house, she counted my newspaper pile, I had twenty-seven New York *Posts*. Poor Norma; she passed away—you know how long?—Tishabov was a year. And last week I started in dialing her number, I wanted to tell her Food of All Nations was having a one-day sale; there was a certain Israeli cheese she was crazy about. . . ."

2

In Dreams Begin Responsibilities

From the notebooks of Chandler Van Horton:

Do they not themselves make jokes of it?
(Viz. *The Passionate People*, Roger Kahn, pp. 21–23, Morrow, 1967)
How they are so ferociously over-organized—i.e., "See here, you are alone on this desert island. Why, wherefore, two synagogues?" "Because the other one I wouldn't go into if they paid me a million dollars."
But still. In Brentwood alone.
JewishAgencyJewishAllianceJewishBundJewishBrother-hood.
JewishCenterJewishCommunity
Three-and-a-half columns.
Murder me for looking.
A telephone directory is not a gas chamber.

In dreams begin responsibilities (Old Play, cited by W. B. Yeats, p. 114, *Collected Poems*, Macmillan, 1945)

Dr. Carolyn Noone
Department of English
Smith College
Massachusetts

Dear Carolyn:
It was during the 1969 MLA meeting

In 1969, Carolyn, you hurt my feelings. It was during
the MLA meeting; you had been hired or as good as hired
by Smith. "Well, let's have a little screw on it," I said. . . .

I am still stung by the remark you made during the
MLA's 1969 meeting—one of their worst, I think. Truly,
Carolyn, I am not now nor have ever been "capable of
abstraction under any circumstance." Indeed, during that
most pleasant act of (your truly first-rate performance of?)
fellatio the "sly academic chuckle" you believe me to have
emitted. . . .

But, Carolyn, when you're right you're right. (Cf. Jules
Farber, *Summa Contra Gentiles*)
For who else, after all, dreams in mastheads . . . ?

And the masthead is my first knowledge of the dream.
I have received in the mail—there is twenty-two cents
postage due—a magazine named *Mogen David*. The cover,
printed on the cheapest stock, announces these articles:
Whither the Jewish Community?, *Wherefore the Jewish
Community?*, *Why a Jewish Community?* and *The Jewish
Community Questions Itself*. But within I can find only a
masthead, and this masthead lists only advisory editors.
Some of these are fixed in my mind with absolute, appalling
clarity: Jacques Barzun, Malcolm Muggeridge, Robert Penn
Warren, Bertrand de Juvenal, Gunnar Myrdal, Lewis Mum-
ford and Alex Rose.

Yet I must have somehow been taken by the magazine,
for I agree to deliver a lecture under its sponsorship. As to
how such agreement is reached and with whom I am unclear, though I have an impression of arduous and artful

negotiations over petty and irrelevant matters. Not once, it appears, is direct mention made of how much I am to be paid—the reasonableness and legitimacy of which I accept, even as I accept the fact that besides lecturing I am to perform some additional unspecified service.

I journey by air—a long flight about which I have little explicit memory save that a fellow passenger, an insane, freakish-looking woman, demands from me some sort of performance. A "Why me?" pops out of my mouth, then a "Why not me?" I will have no trouble, something tells me, none whatever. And I am primed for a dramatic reading from Sholom Aleichem when the woman, at the very moment I am anticipating a stroking of my hair and passionate pinches on my both cheeks, twitches her nostrils like one smelling smoke. Saying, "Never mind, forget it, Lipsky will do it better." The name Lipsky apparently belongs to an enemy, at least to a powerful rival, for I begin arguing that he merely represents the triumph of persistence over talent, that people have really made too much of his few small gifts. "Maybe so," the woman replies, "but he gives very good service." "Talking, ah, speaking of service"—I adopt a disinterested tone, though I am filled with an unaccountable dread—"as to that service. . . ."

But my name is suddenly announced on a loudspeaker, and as I answer "I and Thou". . . "If not now, when?" I enter a place I take to be the lobby of a luxury hotel. There is in the center a magnificent circular desk embellished with intricate carvings depicting the history of the Jews, or so I inexplicably imagine though all I glimpse is the legend *By the waters of Babylon I sat down and wept that I had not bought a little property.* About this desk are a dozen-or-so olive-skinned big-nosed women. One of these women detaches herself and approaches me. "Meals"—she offers a handful of nuts and raisins—"we don't provide on our American plan, but the peerless publicity coverage we got for you you'll never get again."

Next she is smashing me with a black alligator handbag, screaming, "There's no pleasing them, nothing you will ever do for them pleases."

And the other women ring me in.

Each holds a black alligator handbag, each in turn goads me with it, and all together they use me as Indian squaws would use a captive.

They perform an obscene version of the hora; they tell me I have been chosen as door prize for Hadassah; they proffer huge knives and lox in greening malodorous chunks, cackling "Slice it thin! Slice it thin!"; they scourge me with silver foxtails; they offer me waxed fruits and chant "Eat, eat!"; they brandish tinted baby photographs in cut-glass frames; they pluck at the loose skin of my neck, crying out thickly, "Don't tell me this is today's, this is strictly storage stuff!"; they lob whitefish heads and herring skins at my feet; and near my nose they brandish dripping coils of chicken intestines. All the while I remain undismayed, in a state of total indifference—so much so that I cannot even dissemble anger. I am ready to say, in fact, "I am sorry for you, truly sorry. Don't you know—and certainly you should know!—that if I wished, only wished, I could visit upon your heads worse, oh far worse . . . !"

With this I lift my right hand, ready to crook the little finger, aware that for the moment at least it is invested with some awesome power.

But a ram's horn blows one weak note.

Immediately the women, with ballet-like precision, form into a single line and salute me with their handbags. They exit for parts unknown, nicely harmonizing,

> *To Flatbush, to Flatbush*
> *To put on our minks*
> *Home again, home again,*
> *We'll go eat some chinks.*

And I find myself in some sort of surgical amphitheater, standing on an examination table and dressed only in a prayer shawl. Lipsky—and I know it is Lipsky, though he has metamorphosed into Harpo Marx—holds up to my eyes an outsized volume of the Talmud, and I laugh and laugh at him, though lovingly. I tell him, "Lipsky, since when have I had need to refer to the text of our blessed Talmud? Go thou, and do better some small act of charity that you may be pleasing in the sight of God." Then I am seized by a massive excitement, and from this I pass into a state of great contentment and lucidity, as though a mote had been sprung from my eye, a shackle struck from my heart.

"Listen, hear me," I cry to the dense throng in the amphitheater. "Now it *is* said of you people that wisdom has *been* given you, but also that you *shall* know this much and no more, that you be humbled *in* your pride, and thus and so you know *not* the unknowable which is *the* Name of the Nameless, the Power of Powers, the Supreme of Supremes. That Name is *not* for you, unto you It has *not* been given. But see, It has been given me, and I shall speak It—IT!"

I take a deep stiff breath, I open my mouth and I hear the multitude making sounds of fear and weakness.

Only not over me.

For Marlene strides forward, flourishing a brace of horse pistols.

Big and shapely and blonder than in life.

Her eyes the purest baby blue, but holding the darkness of murder.

"Stupid stupid stupid!" she shouts into my face.

I hide myself within the prayer shawl.

"Don't you know?"

I seem to hear Lipsky half-importuning, half-scorning, "Believe what you want to believe."

"He doesn't know," Marlene screams, "that in a moment, the very next moment he would have had to bare his penis for them. Them, them, them!"

I scream back what must have been, could only have

been The Name of Names. And when I battle awake I am still screaming; it takes me some time to recognize my own telephone number.

Postcards from Farber:

Oct. 18

I miss you.
How come I miss you?
Because you have on me a nice effect.
Since you came into my life no more self-hatred.
I can hate you.

Oct. 25

Come already.
How about Tuesday?
You'll help me decide if I'm just cold or if there's a draft in the world.

Nov. 5

Now first I'm getting sore.
I would tell you—you know what I'd tell you?
To kiss my ass and shit in your hat.
Only by you people that's love-play.

Nov. 11

A handwritten note from my Chairman, Professor Buckley

That you have failed to call your mother in 8.2 months is, of course, a personal matter. After speaking with her on the telephone, however, after listening to her tear-crippled voice I took it upon myself to refer her to our college's Social Services Bureau and to offer at once financial aid from the department's Emergency Fund and Contingency Budget line. I suppose, too, that if you see fit to refuse her iodized salt for a massive goiter such con-

duct does not technically fall under our Gross Misconduct or Gross Malfeasance clauses.

What disturbs me, I must confess, is your implied assessment of me both in human and administrative terms. Did you feel that I would have given your curriculum vitae anything less than objective scrutiny if I had known that you were Jewish or that your father performed circumcisions? I am the same man, be assured, who fought so hard after the Six-Day War to bring before the Academic Senate a resolution calling for "whole-hearted congratulations to our colleagues of the Jewish faith."

Nov. 17

With my honors seminar on this day.

Prickly and peevish.

I make the obligatory announcements as though I am being played by Clifton Webb—in a fatigued Oxonian slur of "Snodgrass to read, Cleaver to lecture, Prizes given, Workshop produces, Counseling available, Cafeteria closed. . . ."

I pace the room, hurling bits of chalk, coming at each student with bared teeth.

"Miss Oxblood," I find myself saying, "it is the privilege of youth to be callow; you, however, abuse the privilege."

Two promising discussions I abort. Blaring, "Let us not turn the marketplace of ideas into a discount house," muttering dimly of "the Nubile Left," promising to those who would drop the course double S&H Green Stamps.

I pick up a theme from the desk of Neil Goldenberg— Goldenberg, to whom the very harshest thing I have ever said was "Deeply felt and brilliantly observed." Crying, "Yuck!" I open disdainful fingers, I let it fall and spurn it with a foot. With both feet. . . .

When I hear, as though through endless closed doors, "How long you think you're getting away with it? How long? The whole world is wised up on you, that your Nova Scotia lox comes from Taiwan!"

And we come together in the corridor, Farber and I, like knife and wound.

"Schmuck," he begins.

"When you're right you're right."

"Schmuck, you're such a schmuck, a schmuck like you I need, I need you badly, schmuck."

"You need me, you need me," I grumble out, though my breast is bursting with a beautiful and frightful happiness.

We proceed to punch one another's biceps, at first softly, then with more and more force, swinging like street fighters.

Then we clinch.

"I like my *goyim* cold," says Farber.

"I like my Jews proud and stiff-necked," I answer.

A moment passes.

"You know what I could go for?" Farber dreamily declares. "What I could really, really go for?"

It takes us twenty minutes to travel to a kosher delicatessen, and twenty more till the stuffed derma is ready. By the time Farber has had his third slice—all the while complaining that derma is not in season—I am finished telling him my dream.

Which he interprets as follows. . . .

"It means. . . . It means. . . . I'll tell you what it means: It means you want to get laid."

Then Farber's fingers press on his temple.

"It means also. . . . Also it could mean. . . ."

He tweaks and tweaks my cheeks.

". . . You *got* laid."

Something issues from my mouth; something between sound and speech: A creature cry.

Owlish, avuncular, Farber goes on to say, "She's a bad lay? Believe me, mine Marlene . . ."

"I didn't. I couldn't. I never. Never, never, never, never, never."

"In your 'never,' " he declares, "I hear . . . I hear . . . a 'sometimes.' "

"Fuck yourself," I tell him. "Fuck you."

"Her, fuck *her*," he answers. "With my permission. My permission? My *pleasure*! For my part couple like trains! Link like sausages! Conjugate like verbs! Desecrate her like a synagogue! Hump her, thump her, beat your balls on her ass!"

I wipe at my mouth, at what I believe to be froth. In my thoughts I mount Marlene. While Farber jiggles the mattress, crying, "Now take my wife—please!"

". . . Mixed feelings about you," Farber is saying. "I don't know and I haven't decided if you're prick or if you're cunt. But . . . better you."

A tremor seizes his lips.

"Better you than—"

He looks all at once heavy, thick, dark.

"Why, certainly. I'm no threat. To be sure." I play for time, for laughs. "What, ah, after all, what do I, what would I know from fancy fucking!"

He sets up a tranquilizing murmur of "Ah, ah bay-*bee*," then, raising his voice, "Not that I want her to have it good, but from you she'll have it good. You anyway iron your own shirts, so—so you'll iron her slips. . . ."

I croak out something about servicing her with scholarly journals.

"Because you're the type *goy*—you know what type?"

He nods, continues to nod, and very soon he is rocking.

"You're the type *goy* who doesn't know how to live. But one thing, for one only thing I'll give you credit—"

"Well, well," I mumble vindictively. "There was a time you people . . . cash only."

"Because even if you don't know how to live at least you live by a code. Rules. A yardstick."

"You'd like better"—I rub and rub my hands—"a tape measure?"

He works on me with his eyes, a stern squinting scrutiny in which I behold no humor. "A nice clean *goy*," he says at last, "an immaculate little diamond of a *goy*. With fixed, with regular habits. Give you an Olivetti portable, a one-egg poacher, shoe trees for your three pairs of shoes and we got a happy *goy*. But for a Marlene you're good enough. Because the times . . . they were not made for very dumb twats. And she's at the age and stage. . . . She wants Mr. Wild Stuff. Mr. Dangerous. . . ."

By his long look he draws me into the eye of his mind. Where I seem to see Marlene as he sees her: On iron cots. On flophouse floors. In torture gardens. Attended by implacable horror and nameless evil. The sexual plankton upon which Behemoth studs feed.

"About you," he proceeds placidly, "I wouldn't have to worry."

"Oh yes you would!" I haughtily holler.

"You'd visit her but you wouldn't stay. Which is understandable. After all, you'd miss your foot powder, your Water Pik, your Woolite. And if . . . if you did stay? Maybe one night you're carried away . . . a little touch of gas, and that gas you mistake for surging, for oceanic feelings. On you I could count. No scenes. No roughhouse. Not . . . never with the hands. You'd know there's a kid in the house. You'd know the kid has, he's"—Farber's voice takes flight—"problems. You'd realize, you'd find out he's a very . . . he's quick, he's strong, he moves fast. Zim! Zom! He sees . . . there's a certain coffee table. Heavy, with a heavy marble top. Which you'd cause to one day permanently disappear. With not a word to Marlene that the *bondit* could fall on it, the *bondit* could kill himself. Because that's reality, and for her to cope with reality—by the copers she's no coper. Then, because you'd take an interest in the *bondit*—could you help it? Who could help it?—you'd mix in a little. 'Marlene, dear, divinity, I've noticed the little lad is susceptible to . . . ah, stomach disorders. So even if he starts in . . . with the kicks and the yells . . . don't do what you do. . . .'"

He averts his head.

I avert mine, fix on his last plate of derma, on the side

dish of watery, lifeless peas and carrots. Which I pick up with my fingers. Which I start nibbling crazily, compulsively.

"What she does. This—" is all he can bring forth.

I finish seven peas, four carrots.

"No *potching*," he picks up. "She—she should give him a little slap? That lunk, that clunk, that laziness, that incompetent hunk of shit! Or play with him. Divert him. That's too much like work. If he wants to shine his little flashlight she has to get up, look for it, that means work and—oh, oh, the scene. How she carries on. Can you blame her? After all . . . give in with a flashlight and right away . . . it's the Bambi pull toy. What she does . . . listen what she does. . . ."

Suddenly, stupidly, I flick peas and carrots at him.

"She takes him to the kitchen, she sits him on the floor, on the cold linoleum—that's only when he's wet—and she gives him ice cream. By the half-gallon. Which he can go through . . . the *bondit* . . . a big ten, fifteen minutes. But for those minutes she's free, her spirit can soar. And while her spirit is soaring he does . . . a little accident. Which reminds her she's a mother and a mother has to toilet train, she has to teach the child *sphincter control*. And she controls that sphincter. You know how? You don't want to know—"

"For vegetables you people . . ." I make a vague pushing gesture. "But for children . . ."

All the way back to the campus we quibble and quip, denounce and defend, talking and talking about matters of little moment. In my mail drop I find he has left me a long list of Marlene's favorite positions and perversions. Which is before me as I write these lines.

3

The Vessels
of the Body

Conversations with Marlene
The Second Night

VAN HORTON I want you to give.

MARLENE Tell me to give.

VAN HORTON Marlene, give. Give, Marlene.

MARLENE But if I give . . . oh, say that in this manner and form I give you a satisfaction for the moment. . . .

VAN HORTON Momentary satisfaction. . . .

MARLENE How would you structure it? Would you structure it along the lines of Marlene-is-giving-me-a-fellation-suck?

VAN HORTON Not at all.

MARLENE Can you understand I am not merely going down upon you for an oral-genital caressive act?

VAN HORTON Absolutely.

MARLENE What I now am doing . . . What does it seem I now am doing? Doesn't it seem I have the motivation to only manipulate your scrotal balls?

VAN HORTON Hardly!

MARLENE I happen to believe an individual's balls are part of his essence.

VAN HORTON I feel that way.

MARLENE And to relate to his essence I have to relate to them, I have to . . . *partake* of them.

VAN HORTON Partake, partake.

(An Interval)

MARLENE In saying this . . . it is not to put him down in the sense of belittlement. Two people who have lived together . . . no matter what . . . the vestige remnants have to . . . inevitably . . .

VAN HORTON Inevitably it has to . . .

MARLENE Something is . . .

VAN HORTON It's bound to . . .

MARLENE But at a certain point one must be objective. . . .

VAN HORTON The point of objectivity.

MARLENE Although *total* objectivity . . .

VAN HORTON Who can be . . . ? Which of us has . . . ?

MARLENE But objectively . . . objectively I never liked the taste of his male organ cock.

Conversations with Marlene
The Fifth Night

MARLENE I love burning eyes, and the rabbi had burning eyes.

(Pause)

He had not only burning eyes but he spoke my language. "Marlene, you have, I believe, been brought up in close proximity to nearby farm folk. Perhaps, even, members of your own family performed and engaged in farm work." "You better believe it, Rabbi!" "Marlene, I not only believe it but I likewise believe as well that you are not unfamiliar with the farm folk phrase 'It is a hard row to hoe.'" "I'll say!" "And I suppose, I am confident your mother, in keeping house for your farm family was sensitive to the importance of setting up and maintaining a kitchen of immaculate cleanliness. . . ."

(Pause)

His cash-root indoctrination was to me very persuasively convincing.

(Pause)

I would have done the total conversion thing if I had only to do the cash-root. See, the cash-root . . . they do not have to tell this little old girl about pigs as I have seen a sufficient number of pigs to deem them unclean. Also a shellfish, with or without fins, is to me hateful. So to do the cash-root I could have started with the imaginative fantasy of a pig eating clams. . . .

(Pause)

Oh man, that Mosaic law!

(Pause)

"You see, Marlene, Mosaic law, the law of Moses, applies not solely to the kitchen. Marlene, to quote the words of a teacher far greater than myself, Habooboo Hoohahoo Abahoohoo voo voo voy voy Habooboo." "Rabbi, I do not like the sound of that." "To translate loosely and freely, 'Let the Jewish maiden keep clean the vessels of her kitchen and'—and, Marlene—'the vessels of her body. For there are certain days . . .'

(Pause)

"Well, Marlene, on those days . . . We speak and refer to those days as days of Rabooboo rabeebee abahoohoo voy voy. These are the days, Marlene, when the woman shall not be with the man." "Try and arrange it for a Thursday, Rabbi, as on Thursday Mother Farber likes me to go with her to *Bloomingdale's* . . . ." "During such days, Marlene, the Jewish maiden shall not know her husband. She must baheehoo bahoohee heebahoohoo rebooboo. She shall not permit congress . . . congress or entrance . . . a marital intimacy upon her person by any means . . . by means of or through the medium . . . in no way or in no portion. . . ." "Rabbi, will you please get off my back . . . !"

Conversations with Marlene
The Seventh Night

MARLENE Baby, I hope you are not . . .

VAN HORTON I'm not. Not at all, Marlene.

MARLENE Because . . . and I incidentally say this from no . . . no motivation of fleshly impulse to avoid ruining the night. But as I more and more dwell and linger on that figure, that . . . you said it was six million?

VAN HORTON Six million.

MARLENE I more and more find it acceptable; I accept it.

VAN HORTON That's fine, Marlene.

(Pause)

MARLENE Now what I am puzzled by . . . it beats the shit out of me. . . . Understand, baby, that I not only have granted the six million but I have accepted it; if I didn't accept it my ensuing question would not follow. So. Here. If . . . we have a life loss of six million Jewish people or peoples. Okay. Fine.

(Pause)

But . . .

(Pause)

I am surprised you do not anticipate my question.

(Pause)

Well?

(Pause)

I mean, what had they done?

(Pause)

Look, baby, I am supposed to have the picture that . . .

oh, Hitler and his henchmen . . . they took six million Jewish people or persons and . . . *And* gassing. *And* cremation. *And* inadequate living conditions. All right. Fine.

(Pause)

Look, baby, if that is going to lay a cloudy pall on . . . everything.

I at least can grant it. I grant that they . . . all six million . . . they did nothing.

Conversations with Marlene
The Eighth Night

VAN HORTON *Friend Tim!*

MARLENE *Friend Tim.* In the sight of Christ Therapist I am Friend Marlene and he is Friend Tim.

(Pause)

Oh look, baby . . . this little old girl is *aware.* . . . It is not lost upon me . . . your preference. Naturally. A Freu-oy-oy-dian.

VAN HORTON I would, Marlene.

(Pause)

The most plodding of practitioners. As orthodox as . . .

MARLENE Lox.

VAN HORTON With three-point-two children. I say better, better such a one. . . .

MARLENE And he has a wife: Brenda from brend-dice. Makes sandals. And candles.

VAN HORTON Better, in fact, Rasputin. Oh, let me not say Rasputin. . . .

MARLENE And shopping bag *hendles.*

VAN HORTON Say, rather, Dr. Kronkheit.

(Interval)

MARLENE And she would say, "Marlene, you meant very

well to bake I and Pop ice-box cookies, don't feel griev-
ously hurt that I brought my own food package, we of
course came naturally prepared to depart hungry from
your table, we in fact did not even expect you to have
a table. . . ."

(Pause)

And she would say, "Marlene, I lost the bet and it was
a wager I am happy to lose, I bet Sister-in-Law Lillian
you wouldn't know how to manage a kitchen sink turn-
on, I am pleased my Julie has himself a real hostess
housekeeper. . . ."

(Pause)

And she would say, "I can't get over how you combed
out my hair, Marlene, that was quite a comb-out, this
is the down-to-earth education of practical training they
give secondary high school girls in those villages, they
wisely fit them for what they're fitted, they wouldn't be
happy in our Bergdorf Goodmans, we wouldn't be happy
in their breweries. . . ."

(Pause)

And she would say, "Look how she's upset over a little
miscarriage, a miscarriage everybody gets and everybody
has to live with it, you never know who has them and
who doesn't have them, what does it mean and who
cares, Sister-in-Law Lillian can give the bassinet to Pearl
Rosner, Pearl is the one with five children in three
rooms or three children in five rooms, I am still shocked
Pearl had her perfect pregnancies, all the doctors praised
her perfect pregnancies, I suppose it's a question of the
internal organs, what God wants we don't want, you'd
want Pearl's strong internal organs, Pearl would want
your shapely build. . . ."

(Pause)

And she would say, "Marlene, don't have hurt feelings

if I don't eat your mother's Ukrainian jelly joys, I am
sure your mother meant well, you don't have to tell me
she's a clean little person, in Poughkeepsie Pop and I
were amazed how they washed their hands when they
finished in the outhouse. . . ."

(Pause)

And she would say, "Marlene, all kids get sniffles and
if Mitchee got a sniffle cold he probably was destined to
get a sniffle cold, it has nothing to do with your taking
him out naked in a ninety-mile hurricane wind when
they sent forth an issuance of traveler warnings. . . ."

Conversations with Marlene
The Tenth Night

VAN HORTON Now, Marlene, he'll sleep.

MARLENE I was not hysterical. . . .

VAN HORTON Claimed, however, he couldn't—couldn't or
didn't need to tinkle.

MARLENE I as I see it briefly gave way to my emotions.

VAN HORTON "The Mitchee no tink-tink." But we can be
reasonably confident he tinkled during his nyeh-nyeh.

MARLENE No more, is all.

VAN HORTON He did allow me to put some Desitin on that
urine scald.

MARLENE Those people have wrung or wrested or gotten off
me the last suffering tear of this little dumb old *shikse*
girl. . . .

VAN HORTON Noticed he wasn't at all gassy. Oh, perhaps
the usual pooey or two. . . .

MARLENE Baby, don't worry if I look like I am cupping my
breasts and squeezing my tits.

VAN HORTON But no fever. . . .

MARLENE I am engaged in exercises of respiratory breath-
ing; I through Christ Therapist am only cleansing myself.

VAN HORTON . . . Wouldn't, at any rate, consider ninety-nine-point-two as fever.

MARLENE *Take in me abode, Christ Therapist, fill me, Christ Therapist on or unto my womb....*

VAN HORTON Probably just a bit over-stimulated. . . .

MARLENE . . . And MOVE those hips, *for their seed hath been im- or emplanted in me and I know Thy forgiveness is infinite and it toucheth even the fruit of my womb, it toucheth it surely,* and ST-R-RETCH. . . .

VAN HORTON Although his room isn't as dust-free as I'd like.

MARLENE *Awaken him, thy small servant, from the sleep of mind; let him come unto Thee and by Thee be accepted.*

VAN HORTON And he should have allergen-proof pillow casings and covers.

MARLENE Friend Tim thinks Mitchell has already been accepted; usually one is not accepted unless one does at least a minimum of three immersions in the Healing Fountain.

VAN HORTON *Healing Fountain.*

MARLENE That is why when Friend Tim yelled, "His chest, his chest, look upon his chest!" I did not look; I in fact told Friend Tim not to worry. I said, "Friend Tim, Mitchell since babyhood gets skin eruptions from water; they disappear very quickly; tell him to come out although he will not come out unless you promise him a *Zion is Fallen....*

VAN HORTON *Zion is Fallen.*

MARLENE But Friend Tim and EVERYBODY—"His chest, his chest, behold and gaze. . . ."

VAN HORTON *Healing Fountain and Zion is Fallen. Zion is Fallen and Healing Fountain.* Absolutely. Sure. Why not? What then? This is what Mitch needs, he needs this badly, more than this he doesn't need. . . .

MARLENE And I gazed on his chest and I *beheld....*

VAN HORTON All right. Okay. Sense I didn't look for. Who looked for sense? I looked for sense? Sense you don't have and you have no sense. But a heart! A mother shouldn't have a heart? Have a little heart, you crazy cunt, realize who you're dealing with. Do you realize who you're dealing with . . . ?

MARLENE I at least *think* I beheld it. I would have liked to *gaze* upon it. . . .

VAN HORTON This is the *bondit!*

MARLENE I, however, shall take Friend Tim's word. I mean . . . look, baby, it wasn't stigmata or anything, just a little old sign of the cross. . . .

VAN HORTON The *bondit*, the *bondit*, the *bondit*. . . .

4

Camp Ground

Even now, some three years after Farber's death, I am dogged by earnest graduate students who, following the fashion not only of the titans of trivia but of the most serious-minded scholars, explicate and extol Farber as a deeply representative figure of our cynical seventies, one whose life, especially in its last stage, underscores society's persistent persecution of the unorthodox. He has been viewed, alternately, as "a ritual scapegoat taking upon himself the sorrows of us all" (Marion Foglia, *At Once*, Spring, 1974); as a "supreme locker room bully flicking the wetted end of his towel at the exposed backside of capitalism" (I. M. Lacey, *Nay-Sayer*, October, 1974); as the one comic artist "who managed to place himself at the precise point between culture and anarchy" (Nathanael Picauer, *Avant-Garde and Kitsch*, January–February, 1974).

Two recent studies—*Jesters and Jeremiahs*, by Nadia R. Spiegelman, Chanticleer Press; and *America: Land of the Sad Clown*, by Jerold Insdorf, Arden and Dale—show, among other things, that it is time, high time, for scholars to stick their heads out the ideological window for a few simple breaths of philistine fact. I say this with no great joy, for Spiegelman and Insdorf, despite a shared tendency to strain after verbal and philosophic effects—i.e., Professor Insdorf's solemn-silly comments about "alienated insiders"—offer, each in his own way, shrewd and sympathetic insights into the roots and reaches of Farber's genius. Granted, Mrs. Spiegelman is not exactly the first to break the big news about "the comic's eternal war with inanimate objects"; nor should Professor Insdorf have been quite so quick to locate "the green pastures of Grossinger's *right off* (italics mine) the New York State Thruway."

And from baby blunders Professor Insdorf moves by giant steps to massive misinterpretation. I shall mercifully overlook his wilder, weirder speculations, though some take an awful lot of overlooking. (Samples: "To Farber, the form of Orthodox Judaism was its content" . . . "He was to learn that the Catskills were, after all, a far cry from Sholom Aleichem's Kasrilevke" . . . "For the sensitive Jewish adolescent the candy store functioned as a kind of sacred grove.") Said speculations, I should add, are accompanied by a tendency to work and worry at points no more difficult to grasp than bananas. Apropos of movies, Professor Insdorf solemnly reminds us that they "doubtlessly played a vital role in Farber's formative years"; then, some three paragraphs later, commits himself to "movies must certainly have enriched Farber's fantasy life."

But after such hesitation over the humdrum, after confronting the commonplace with awesome objectivity, Professor Insdorf turns oddly assertive. Propositions at best tentative, at worst downright absurd, are suddenly calcified into doctrine and dispensed as a higher form of wisdom. Thus, it is as impossible to validate as it is to vitiate his notion that the true comic artist "can ill afford the luxury of being at home in his age"; indeed, what can one say of this point, which belongs somewhere in the middle range between pious platitude and illuminating insight? Or how, for that matter, is one to handle the sweep, the smugness, the sweeping smugness, of his "America, of course, has never been hospitable to its first-rate talents"?

Now despite my nagging and needling I am aware, believe me, of how delicate and difficult a task it is to "locate" Farber—so delicate, so difficult, that one wonders if he can or should be placed at all. For every classification is fitting, yet none precisely fits. We can exalt him, like Logan Levy in *Esquire*, June, 1974 ("at least the funniest man the Jewish middle class is ever likely to produce"); exalt and diminish him simultaneously like *Time*, October 16, 1974 ("A man for all seasons—especially the fifth season"), yet we seem never to say just what we wanted to say.

And just what was it Professor Insdorf wanted to say? Something, to be sure, about Farber, about his kind and why he was special among that special kind. Such is Professor Insdorf's avowed intent, set down at the outset. ("I hope here to examine a number of the larger social implications arising out of Farber's rediscovery—a rediscovery which cannot be explained by the mere fact that he was a highly gifted entertainer, quite possibly more than that." Well, one is entitled to ask, I suppose, if that fact is, after all, such a "mere" fact. But Professor Insdorf is out to make a statement, one that is serious and significant and universal, and apparently it is hard to make such a statement about a man engaged in what is essentially a low-brow enterprise—I say "apparently" because Professor Insdorf goes to great pains to explain or explain away the means by which Farber earned his living.

Not once, for instance, is Farber plainly called a stand-up comic. On page 19 he is a "vertical monologist" who, by page 24, makes it as a "powerful parodist" only to be brought down, on page 26, into the ranks of the "irony-mongers." Such eccentric euphemisms, frequently funny and always fatuous, abound. Instead of emcee, Professor Insdorf prefers "host to the homogenized"; poor Ed Sullivan—at least I *think* he means Ed Sullivan—turns out to be "the

featureless hierophant of kitsch"; Mike Douglas is "Mister
Mass Mind"; the Borscht Belt becomes "that midcult-and-
suit meadowland"; gagwriters are "shlocksmiths"; and a
comic walks out upon a nightclub floor "to effect a liaison
with the lumpen. . . ."

Never mind.

Professor Insdorf, let us remember, intends to say something with "larger social implications," something that will
provoke us to reflect about . . . Farber? Oh, Farber of course,
though not *exactly* about Farber, never Farber in particular
or a particularized Farber. More, much more important to
him is the "phenomenon" of Farber, the "question" of Farber, the "issue" of Farber. These are the only matters which
his method permits—a method which, depending on one's
point of view, can be regarded as vulgar Marxism or good
sociological criticism. Still, if I do not exactly venerate this
method, I believe I can understand and sympathize with
the reasons that may have led Professor Insdorf to choose it.

For it seems to me that no intellectual can overcome a
certain feeling of homelessness in the province of the popular arts or suppress altogether that Farberesque voice eter-
nally demanding, "Who asked for you and who sent for
you; who sent for you and who asked for you?" Neither
precepts nor precursors are there to guide him as he makes
his agonizing effort to achieve an accommodation with his
subject, to certify its legitimacy in the household of art, to
find new ways of writing and thinking about it.

We will need another Aristotle, I imagine, another kind
of *Poetics* to even deal adequately with these problems, let
alone solve them—and I make no such demands of Professor
Insdorf or of his study. All the same it is reasonable to expect that somewhere along the way he would have conceded
their existence, indicated that they were on his mind, given
for a moment, only a moment, evidence that he can, in
Farber's words, "at least—and this is the least—*aggravate* a
little."

But he has his method, a method which, I daresay, is

seductive. For its inexorable laws and logic protect him against the assault of actuality—the actuality, say, of a complex, contrary flesh-and-blood Farber, a Farber whose life and works might fail on occasion to provide "a text of our fearful, broken moral order," whose character and motives obstinately defy encapsulation within "the arena of public struggle," whose fate, finally, claims our attention as a human fate and not because it is "a parable of martyrology."

And Mrs. Spiegelman, like Professor Insdorf, is never at a loss for comment, never caught without a catch-phrase. But if both scholars serve the same method, it must also be said that Mrs. Spiegelman is a less impersonal writer, that she gives us now and again glimpses of a Farber who has not been zapped by the *Zeitgeist*. Throughout, she seeks to do him justice, and passage after passage is suffused with compassion for the man; alas, I doubt that the man is necessarily Farber.

Thus, we have enough cause, as I hope to show later, for moaning, maybe ululating over Farber's problems; whatever these were, though, they did not include "a longing for death to heal his profound emotional rifts." In fact, Dr. I. Marvin Lubash, his personal physician, has called him "the IT and T of hypochondria," claiming that Farber even owned his own sphygmomanometer. But misty-eyed and suffused with melancholy, Mrs. Spiegelman advances to her next proposition, namely that Farber "had not sufficiently hardened himself against the possibility of failure." He hadn't, I suppose, any more than I, Mrs. Spiegelman or most of the population of the continental United States. Much depends, though, upon the definition of failure, and I am frankly still puzzled by Mrs. Spiegelman's. How broad it must be to ingest a comedian whose bookings upon his death could have carried him easily through the next five months! Conceivably this is a small matter, a matter of emphasis, I told myself, after doing a double-take—only to suffer a slow burn from the following. . . .

". . . Paraphrasing Joyce, he was Jewish, all too Jewish—

too Jewish for the general public, at times even for a Jewish public. A day of reckoning was close at hand, a day when his intransigence would cost him dearly, for he had been at best profligate with his moral and material resources, *a poor caretaker of his career . . ."* (italics mine).

Farber, I have said elsewhere, had his own phrase for academics: "*Yentas* with facts"; I hope I do no disservice to his memory by insisting that in Mrs. Spiegelman's case he was only half-right.

For this "intransigent," this "profligate," this "poor caretaker of his career" left an estate whose assets—see Public Docket #5961–27, California State Supreme Court, Division of Probate, Alma Heidi Strug Acting Chief Clerk—consisted, in cash alone, of $343,571.79. Some other holdings which might have deferred that "day of reckoning. . . ."

A one-third interest in the *Butterfinger Bakeshop,* Port Washington, New York.

A non-voting partnership in *Pinocchio Day Camps, Inc.,* Howard Beach, Brooklyn.

Two franchises, one of which had been exercised, for *Mister Malted* stands in North Philadelphia.

Options held in trust for Mitchell Robert Farber on undeveloped properties in Bergenfield, New Jersey, said properties managed by Lagunoff Realtors and known as the *Eat, Eat Corporation.*

Twelve-and-a-half percent holdings in *God's Country Recreation Village,* a subsidiary of Livealittle Associates, Lefrak City, Queens.

It must have been around this point that feelings of frustration overwhelmed me. However broad or charitable my view, however often I excused Mrs. Spiegelman's fashionable fictions, her tendency to seek complex explanations when simple ones would serve, I began sensing, at bottom, a purpose, an intent which her method alone failed to explain. Yet not till her penultimate chapter, I confess, did I get glimmerings of what she was about.

Those two epigraphs, for example. . . .

*For the thing which I greatly feared is come upon me,
and that which I was afraid of is come unto me.*
Job 3:25

*For years . . . Eisenstein has been working as if in a prison,
under the supervision of jailers who are not only peculiarly
dangerous and merciless but also as sudden to change their
minds as minnows their direction. . . .*
James Agee, On Film

Was she preparing us, I wondered, for a portentous announcement or a spell of sobbing? A bit of both, as it turns out.

"All the elements of tragedy," she begins, "combined to color the close of his life."

And here I had, somehow I had a hunch whom Mrs. Spiegelman was to identify as the villains of this tragedy.

"It was not lost upon The Moneymen (her caps) that new, dangerous qualities had surfaced in Farber's art—qualities that combined to render it less manageable and marketable. During the late fifties and most of the sixties Farber's comic character had been a construction of willful wackiness resting on an obsessive but engaging premise: When you're in love the whole world is Jewish; and perhaps, in fact, even when you're not in love.

"With the Nixon era, however, the easygoing ecumenicism of the past decade began eroding. The whole world, Farber saw all too clearly, was not Jewish, and those whom he had long scorned as 'pork loins,' as the 'Big Macs,' sat in the seats of power and set the tone of the times. If they were every bit as cruel as he believed them to be—'You'll shoot at them rubber bands and they'll shoot back real bullets'— they were also more cunning than he had imagined. The comic artist in him they could afford to ignore, but the moralist who spoke through him—'I have seen the future and it works on my nerves'—had to be subdued and silenced. This they would finally accomplish—on May 3, 1972, to be exact, when Farber's very last appearance before a television camera was summarily, mysteriously, withdrawn from broadcast."

Well, someone was bound to displace Lenny Bruce in the liberal imagination, and I suppose we shall be hearing for years to come of the censoring and scissoring of Farber, of how he was "subdued and silenced." Wasn't he? After all, the fact is—isn't it a fact?—that Farber's very last guest shot *was* withdrawn—"summarily, mysteriously."

Mysteriously?

By no means.

For it was the times, just one of the signs of the times, infers Mrs. Spiegelman, and I have no quarrel with the way in which she has read those signs. But I do wish she had managed to read simultaneously and among other materials an occasional copy of *Video*—the issue, say, of May 6, 1972, containing this item from the *Here's Herman* column. . . .

"Under the *Go Plotz* Dep't:

"No, viewers and victims, you're not crazy . . . last Thursday's Ricky Shane Show didn't hang right conner 22 of those 90 minutes got lopped. . . . Why them missing minutes? Seems like guester-jester Jules Farber had the effrontery (*chutzpah*) to become late Jules Farber right between show's taping and telecasting. . . . When obit hit wire services the ganza-sponsor (Oneida Farmland Mutual) hit ceiling and gave network takeout order. 'Nothing personal,' Oneida-guider and author of defective directive Harry P. Kelso told me, 'only it must be understood that Mr. Farber's posthumous appearance would have cast grave and serious doubts upon the corporate message we have sought to stress and emphasize these several years: Oneida Sells Life!' . . . You're all heart, Mr. Kelso, and up your actuarial table. . . ."

I see no reason to believe, though, that reading the above would have swayed Mrs. Spiegelman in the slightest; as I have said already, she is compassionate and generous-hearted, insisting upon the sorrows of Farber as strongly as Professor Insdorf insists upon the contradictions of capitalism. And for these sorrows she holds responsible—whom or what does she *not* hold responsible? Great gobs of blame go flying to fall, during the last several pages, upon Madison Avenue and Wall Street, teen-agers and golden-agers, the debasement of public taste and the public taste for debasement, the human condition in general and the American character in particular. But if the victimizers are splattered, so too is the victim.

" 'Love me, love me, love me,' " writes Mrs. Spiegelman, "was the Farber demand. It is the demand all great clowns have issued, and the audience has always acceded as long as certain conditions be met—as long, that is, as W. C. Fields remains the dirty old man, Chaplin the Little Tramp, Lenny Bruce the impudent improvisor. But give us, this audience demands in turn, only what we are equipped to handle. Do not confuse us by stepping out of character, by seeking to show us, under the clown's mask, a Falstaff, a Monsieur Verdoux, a philosopher-king of the potheads.

"But ultimately Farber, like Fields, like Chaplin, like Bruce, damaged, perhaps destroyed the delicate rapport between himself and his audience, asking of them, as John Friedman puts the matter, 'not love or laughter alone, but something beyond love and laughter; at the end he was to receive neither.'

"How could he? one may conjecture.

"For years Farber's best routines had been italicized by spite ('On this day,' he would quote from the secret repressed diary of Anne Frank, 'I applied by Bloomingdale's for a charge account!') Then, as his life and expectations ebbed ('The price of egg creams is thirty-five cents now,' he gloomed, taking off on Lloyd George, 'we shall not see them lowered in our time') as he worked closer and closer to the dangerous edge of the permissible ('Sure they'll beat their swords into ploughshares . . . and then, then first they'll give it to you with those ploughshares'), as he one by one rejected the assumptions upon which our world rests, he took measures compelling the world to reject him in turn. It may be that we have no recourse save to hold with John Friedman, who makes this point:

" 'He must surely have known what he was about, known that he was donning his own hair shirt, driving the nails into his own flesh. In the best of times, it has been said, the annihilating, corrosive savagery Farber manifested on the Ricky Shane Show might have easily compelled cancellation of his segment—and these are not the best of times. . . .' "

How annihilating, how corrosively savage Farber must have been may be estimated by the following editorial (my thanks to Vera Mehrtens of the Ricky Shane staff for providing me with a copy) which appeared originally in the *Pebble Beach Temple Newsletter*, May 14, 1972. . . .

A Swell Guy Gone
Gone is a swell guy; deceased is Jules—to us, Julie—Farber.

Many things he was to many men, but to all men he was—a mensch.

During all his too few years Jules Farber's life gave living proof of the simple truth upon which stands the superstructure of our Judeo-Christian ethic: That only when people act like people can a person be a person.

Our story follows here.

Here follows our story.

The undersigned quintet of Jewish women had in its collective possession five (5) tickets to the Ricky Shane Show—tickets which it had requested by writing no less than eight (8), no more than ten (10) weeks prior to receipt of same.

Came the appointed night and this quintet of Jewish women took places on the line—a long line and a slow-moving line. After an hour's wait, said quintet managed to effect admission.

With spirited unity, with the high resolve to situate itself together, the undersigned quintet of Jewish women secured frontal row placement.

Elation and contentment dominated the moods of the five (5); the general feeling was summed up as "A good time will be had by all."

But down the aisle came an usher who in manner of rough crudeness informed us, for reasons still unclear, that we must yield up the seats to others.

Our reply was simple.

Simply we replied, and the reply was "No."

And we set forth the reasons for our refusal; namely that the usher now must reckon with new aspects of the Jewish character—a prideful militancy, a steely determination, a heightened consciousness born from the realization that Jews must link their aspirations to the ongoing struggle for human and civil rights being waged by those hitherto deprived of their rightful place on the socioeconomic ladder.

The time has come, the moment is at hand, we asserted, for the making of waves—for an awareness on the part of Jews everywhere that they must leave behind a fragmented value system and assist others toward a full, fair share of their democratic heritage.

The disputation grew heated.

Heated grew the disputation.

So heated, in fact, that the undersigned quintet of Jewish women did not at first realize that the "warm-up" of the studio audience had begun.

Nor were they aware Jules Farber himself had bounded off the stage till he stood in their midst—till he was berating the belligerent usher, gently chiding him thusly. . . .

"Don't—don't be hard on him, folks. The kid got terrible news, the kid got dreadful news. Because only today they threw his mother out of the Lutheran Home for the Aged; she forgot to drop her G's."

A moment later he moved on.

He moved on a moment later.

First, though, he gazed genially upon the undersigned quintet of Jewish women. And he softly inquired if he was correct in his surmise, if the fact of our Jewishness were indeed a fact.

"Yes," we answered in a collective voice of muted mildness.

"Never never never be ashamed you're Jewish," he admonished us. "Because it's enough if I'm ashamed you're Jewish."
Therefore we say. . . .
We say therefore. . . .
A swell guy is gone.
Gone is a swell guy.

by
Natalie (Ramona) Chutick, Leda LeVien, Eugenie Daroff,
Myrna Turtletaub and Georgette Glassman

From this "undersigned quintet of Jewish women" at least, Farber drew no more blood than they were willing to lose. Doubtlessly I make too much of their tribute: At most and at best they are representative, in Farber's term, of *Yiddle* America, and perhaps even that is an excessive claim for them. In any case, they seem to show themselves as obtuse, thick and impenetrable. Are they not aware, one keeps thinking, surely they must be aware that Farber was using and abusing them?

Or—this thought intrudes into the forefront of my mind —perhaps they had not mistaken a karate chop for a lovetap. Perhaps, indeed, the rapport between Farber and his audience was not quite as delicate as Mrs. Spiegelman believes it to have been.

I will not press the point, nor do I have any irrefutable argument to advance on its behalf. For one thing, Farber's audience is not before us, for another, we can never know exactly what transaction any comic ever makes with any audience. Only this much is hard, fixed, intractable: No matter how much damage the comic does during his five fast minutes it is he who must receive the pie in the face, the kick in the behind.

And Farber received the pie, the kick—from whom and under what circumstances is a matter I shall address myself to later, and in some detail. But the miracle and mystery of Farber's genius all along resided, I believe, in his ability to simultaneously honor and humiliate, to kiss and to kill, to keep us thrillingly balanced between security and despair. That, as Mr. Friedman declares, he was "donning his own hair shirt, driving the nails into his own flesh" is perceptive and incontestable. I believe Farber's audience was aware of this, had always been aware. I believe, however, that they were deeply and unshakably convinced, far more so than even Farber believed them to be, that in him they confronted what "the undersigned quintet of Jewish women" called a *mensch*—the lovely Yiddish word meaning one who is truly human; a person; a truly human person.

This conviction, I would insist, endured and prevailed during Farber's segment on the Ricky Shane Show. For I was there; I was informed of Farber's mood and condition (would I had been less well informed!); and I have examined and re-examined every single one of his lines syllable by syllable, every last bit of business gesture by gesture, checking my own copious notes a dozen times over against the videotape. Each time I have caught his "demand for something beyond love and laughter," each time complying, and with all my heart.

I like to think I complied that night; at times, in fact, I catch myself creating comforting fictions, mythologizing the smallest matters. Was there something special to be observed in his slow-kindling smile that day? Did he take my hand somewhat more willingly, grasp and knuckle it a shade too long? Might not his greeting of "*Nu*, schmuck . . . ?" have been purged of its customary querulousness? To be sure, I recollect a shortness of breath as he stooped over his shoes, an air of weakness and fatigue and a distinct ineptitude with the laces and knots—yet things had always seemed to fall from his hands. For that matter his large chest and breadth of shoulder were deceptive, giving the illusion, but only the illusion of great strength.

Nor do I detect anything prodigious in my notes for the next hour. *Marlene*—I find her name three times circled and the vowels savagely blackened—*references to*. I suppose, thinking upon it, that I might better have perceived how very much Farber was aroused against her, might have made some stronger effort to shed my old self, my scholar's temperament, meeting suffering with suffering: What Farber needed were death shrieks; what I could give him was "Gently, gently, guy" and "Easy, easy, sport."

Besides which, he was putting us in danger, literally in danger of our lives. For we were in a studio limousine and the driver, held up near the MacArthur Freeway by a funeral procession, now was concentrated exclusively on making time, moving at fearful speeds, blasting his horn, straddling lanes to crowd trucks that looked to me as long as locomotives, accelerating from abrupt pitching stops like an arrow leaving a bow. While Farber, balanced on the jump seat, would seek to distract him.

Croaking "Pizza pizza" into the man's ear.

Saying, "You're an Italian kid, right? Am I right? I can tell, you know how I can tell? Because you got no neck."

Pre-human cries were released from him during the next few perilous moments: *Like elephant bulls smelling the white hunter,* my notes read, *like Grendel entering a mead hall.*

Next he had a blank check in his hand and he was thrusting this check at the driver and teasing his nostrils with it.

Here, I believe, I must have tasted his darkness, here I must have muttered my "Gently, gently, guy" and my "Easy, easy, sport" and my other cries of fear and weakness.

For he wanted Marlene dead.

He was freakish, ludicrous, crazed, operatic, satanic, self-delighted, posturing, but also he was in earnest.

By his weeping voice, by his flawed timing, by the milky murderous fluids that consumed the light in his eyes I knew.

But I believed what Farber had willed himself into believing: That he was only doing his comic's work.

As he pleaded, "You'll make on her a nice hit. Something—*vino, vino!*—clean, quick, easy. Because I don't want suffering and she shouldn't have to suffer. All right, maybe

—and it's up to you, it's in your hands—two, three weeks of mortal agony."

As he offered five hundred dollars and twenty-five cents —"the twenty-five cents in case you should feel like ices"— for each pulverized bone in her extremities; if, further, it was no bother and no imposition he would appreciate special attention to her pelvic girdle. ("You could work on it with Sicilian salamis.")

As he reduced his demands to single, only a single eviscerated organ, though a major one, simultaneously begging the driver for the names of his nearest and dearest so that he might choose for them some little gifts: A Hoffritz tweezer for his mother's mustache; a wrist-band for his father; an acne transplant for his sister.

As he fended off imaginary blows and, twitching so hard I could hear the crack of vertebrae, wailed, "Hey, Auntie Pearlie."

As he spoke or seemed to speak with her, saying softly, "Oh, you hurt me good. You didn't want to come to the wedding? Answer, 'No,' or 'No, thank you.' Ah, but that 'Absolutely not' was high-horse stuff which I didn't have coming to me."

As he broke off, begging the driver for a look at the family ice pick, then resumed, saying, "Believe me, though, you were right, Auntie Pearlie. Kiss a pinkie and so help me God, you called it good. 'Go, go and buy for her Christmas trees.' Because let me tell you: I went; I bought; and from one year to the next they got bigger. And don't think it ended there. Nah, not at all, oh no. Listen, I had to miss your unveiling; this was her condition if I wanted the *bondit* to have a *brith*. And you don't know what I had with her for Cousin Mattie's wedding. She wouldn't go unless . . . three months, for three months I was not allowed to call Mom and Pop. But this she is not. . . . Oh no, no, no. . . . Now this she won't live to get from me, before I give in on this, I can tell you, believe me, I swear. . . ."

He suddenly said, "So?"

I said, "*Nu?*"

He looked into my eyes.

I looked away from his.

And remained silent, coldly silent.

Thinking, silently grumbling. "Well, what do you want of me? Please. Ye gods. Bear in mind our differences. This far I can go, but only this far. I am of colder stock, aged and seasoned in Puritan brine. I am center, not periphery. I was made for surfaces, not for the terrors of the underground. Do you know that when I was twelve I stole a canoe and disappeared for two days, covering forty-five miles of terrible white water? A rain-swollen tributary where guides —guides, I say!—had capsized. Yes, with a broken nose and three broken toes I came into the house, but my father said only, "Well, hello there. . . .""

Farber said, "So?"

I said, "*Nu?*"

He said, "Friends."

I said, "*Chaverim.*"

He said, "Best friends."

I said, "Toklas and Stein, Brod and Kafka, Falstaff and Hal, Laurel and Hardy."

I believe, I will always believe that I would have said more, that near Burbank, in fact, my nostrils were flaring, my mouth working and working to deliver my hidden feelings. "My mother . . . ," I shakily began, meaning to tell him that she'd done a thing or two to me as a child. "Why in her way," I had in mind, "she buffaloed and oppressed me with her notions about firm and responsible character. At six I was feeding myself on a dollar a day. Yes, and at nine I had the job of walking my crazy great-aunt Christine round and round the playground. She believed she was nanny to the children of Queen Victoria, and I would have to call them with her. 'Come Alfred, come Edward, now Leopold, at once Alice and Louise.' While she boxed my ears and cracked my head with that heavy ivory fan."

But he wished to spare me.

He wished to spare me or to put me on notice, perhaps, that man is not so easily turned into *mensch*.

I cannot otherwise account for the "Shah. Shah-shah-shah," that burst from his lips, for the way he opened and closed his hands and made gestures of negation.

Or for the task he set me at the studio.

I insist it was a task, and I report on it without shame.

I report too that I was at the time altogether lucid, though my spirit was very open and in a state of purest happiness.

And so when I was lumbering behind Farber on the midway of the stage and he all at once smiled barbarically and clasped arms about my middle I was ready; perhaps I had always been ready.

Lifting as he leaped, carrying him past the baffled grips and electricians, the sad-faced writers testing out their gags, the hard-eyed chorines grousing like truck drivers as they shaved their body hair, the choreographer chalking the floor in his tight provocative pants, the band going "Yum yum" and extending limp wrists.

I am told Farber bawled, "Thank God I don't have to walk!," that I bawled, "*First* we'll try the Wailing Wall—*then* Lourdes!"

For I must have been momentarily out of my head, hearing only with skin, nerves, spirit a run of gross yet lovely laughter. Stay with it, I remember thinking, turn on, man, *mensch*, this is the real stuff—the universal belly laugh.

I should say also that I could not hold on long to the feeling, let alone to Farber. But while it lasted I would have worn for him cap and bells or grown a bear's coat and snout to dance a hora.

Then what matter if I figure this day as the probable origin of my slipped disc?

And though I bumped Farber's head against a musician's stand, though my knees, my organs, started slowly to sink and I poured sweat and saliva, I did not set him down before he produced certain characteristic high, sweetly nasal cantorial sounds whereby I judged his tension broken.

"Oh, you pro," I inwardly hailed him, "you top banana, you magnificent monster," as he restored himself by goosing, by hiking skirts, by trumpeting "Oomgawah" and "Methadone, methadone!" at the black drummer.

And about this time, I believe, I spoke my last significant words to him.

These were: "Where did Dr. Kildare practice? I remember where he practiced—"

Who can say if he heard my "Blair General Hospital!" or if he had other reasons to take my neck in a wrestling grip and knock our brows together softly? "Oish-oish-oish," he hissed, pulling and pinching my ears. Though I answered only "Heh Heh," I was on the verge of "See?" and "Wasn't I with it?" and "The little *goy* who could." But buzzers went off, microphones and monitors came alive and we were immediately conducted to a hot and close room furnished in—I use Farber's phrase—early dispensary. Here, under naked bulbs, amid empty water bottles, stacked folding chairs, cartons holding liquid soap and other lavatory stuff, sat the day's guests, glum, formal, covering nervous yawns.

And Farber, predatory, persecuting, but also benevolent, as though performing some ancient duty, went among them.

To Father Francis Walsh, the Paulist priest, he said, "Hey, I hear there's a lot of clap in the parish!" and "Whatever happened to the Twin Cantors?"

To Marcy Maley, the starlet, he said, "You had trouble getting here, right? Am I right? You were on your way, you got into a taxi but from force of habit you started hemorrhaging."

To Richard Pomerantz, author of *No, He's My Brother*, he said, "Give me your tired, your poor, your hungry masses yearning to breathe free—and I'll make a fortune from costume jewelry."

Next he was sucking breath.

He was sucking breath and bowing low to the floor.

True, he converted this into a pratfall, and by his comic's instinct came up capering and prancing.

But death must must have been speaking through him.

With eloquent spasms of tachycardia, with fibrillation and constricting vessels.

"Pain?" Dr. I. Marvin Lubash was to tell me. "Well, if a cute little mole started burrowing in his chest and a cute little eagle tried to get at the cute little mole and the cute little eagle had this very dull beak. . . ."

Nevertheless Farber stormed, positively stormed onstage for the warm-up. He had not been scheduled, and so the announcer, Bud McVeety, at first failed to comprehend the two-fingered whistles, the violence of the laughter. But then he very shrewdly let himself be converted into Farber's mind-less instrument—raising his hands with practiced helpless-ness, blinking and squinting, showing on his face only aggrieved innocence and deep sweet vulnerability.

Then with a "Shah. Shah-shah-shah" Farber stilled the audience, drawing all eyes to the large bandanna he was plucking off McVeety's neck.

He first held this bandanna aloft slowly, then very slowly tied at each corner a pair of lumpy knots.

And he fitted it over his head and with swift skill sculpted it into the effigy of a skullcap.

There followed a dance.

It has been said the dance was a spoof, a parodic blend of Hasidic and rock movements; and some, principally Ty Kaplan, then Ricky Shane's head writer, recognized in Far-ber's melodious croaking sustained snatches of the *Bonanza* theme. But I am compelled to offer these disjointed frag-ments from my notes.

For I hold the view that Farber was addressing God.

Thusly . . .

Thy rod and thy staff they clobber me.

I call upon You—and how often do I call upon You?— and from the answering service I get "No more Mr. Nice Guy" or "I don't need the business."

But there was a time You took an interest; You showed a little initiative.

All right, we had a few bad years, but who counts?

Yea, You promised us; Yea, You were putting together this terrific act for us: Yea, we'd open with the commandments; Yea, one-liners like the commandments you don't hear these days.

All right; okay; let it pass.

But if we ask You, oh Big Shot—and don't we have a right to ask You?—"Where, where did it go wrong?" don't answer, "Look, it went beautiful in rehearsal."

I have spoken of this dance with Don Rickles, pressing the claim that Farber was in an inspired condition—"As though," I recall bringing out, "God were beating him with a pig bladder." "Pig bladder," Rickles answered fervently. "Eh-heh. Inspired condition. Eh-heh eh-heh eh-heh." He backed off by inches, fingering the Star of David at his throat. And Alan King, after announcing, "As soon as I finish his cigar I'm going to feel such a nameless existential dread!" went on to say, "I'll tell you the story of why I don't interpret. Why don't I interpret? Because one time in high school I had this substitute for English. Mr. Simick or Mr. Simitz. And Mr. Simick or Mr. Simitz one day comes in, sits down and shoots at us two lines. *Tiger, tiger burning bright/In the forests of the night.* And again the two lines. *Tiger, tiger burning bright/In the forests of the night.* And he gets up and he paces for a minute and while he's pacing he shoots at us a question: 'Who, now who can tell me why Blake put down the lines that way and not another way?' Immediately my mouth is open and I yell a very snappy 'Because they sounded good to him!' 'Repeat that!' 'Because they sounded good to him!' To which Mr. Simick or Mr. Simitz makes reply, 'You know, you're absolutely right—but you ought to hear some of the crazy answers I get.' "

But Rickles and King and even Buddy Hackett with his croaky commentary ("Either you read too many *Cahiers du Cinéma* or too many *Tillie and Mac* books") concede the point I would now make: That when the show was some eight minutes underway and Farber left Ricky Shane suddenly, spectacularly alone onstage to descend into the audience this was not (1) "symbolic comment on the shallow, venal merchandiser Ricky Shane had become" (Isa Kapp, *New Leader*, January 17, 1973); or (2) "a low-brow equivalent of Mallarmé's blank page" (Ezra Rosenberg, *The Minotaur*, December 3, 1973); or (3) "an announcement that the uneasy marriage between Kasrilevke and cashbox was at an end" (Vera Herbstmann, *The Jewish Week*, February 23, 1973).

Which is not to say all was *gemütlichkeit* and affectionate razzing between Farber and Shane. A certain coolness, a mild constraint had developed, Shane told me on the day of Farber's funeral. "You'll hear it's because my wife threw him out of the house," he declared. "She did not throw him out of the house. She had him escorted from the premises. 'Suh, yawl will be ass-coated from these yere premises.' 'You want I should go?' 'And be day-yummed to yuh, suh.' 'I hope your whole body turns into a vestigial organ. . . .'"

Nor was his wife altogether at fault. For she had been catering to Farber all that afternoon, going back and forth from the pool to fetch him tall glasses of Dr. Brown's Cel-Ray and mixed platters of the cold cuts he generally favored. Yet Farber simply sat and sat, unsmiling, with an air of grievance and distraction. Till a call came from his answering service; he was to immediately phone a certain Rabbi Figtree. In chambers. Using the special Confidence Line. And though Farber had fled to the farthest cabana his voice carried. He sounded bitterly angry; he sounded as though he knew he could not afford anger. There was first some flip, flutey "Rabbi dears" and "Rabbi honeys," followed by shouts of forced laughter. "See her, go see her. It's your busy season, I know, you have to start preparing the Yom Kippur cookout, but go and see her." Then, "Hey. HEY! Don't give me your social work schlock. 'This lies outside muh pur-voo and jar-isdiction.' But an all-night vigil for Caesar Chavez—that, that already is *within* your puhvoo and jar-isdiction." Well, nothing, oh not the "Cock-sucker!" or the "Fucking Bastard" had offended Shane's wife as mightily as the reference to Chavez. Hot-faced and near tears, she nevertheless had held back, waiting till Farber had finished eating before saying she could not decide whether he needed scolding for his anti-Semitism or his anti-unionism. Farber muttered something about her need-ing either multiple orgasms or multiple contusions, and the trouble began.

Therefore Shane had anticipated a rough time from Farber. And so what? And why not? A little excess, a little . . . Easternism would be good for the show, good for him. Never mind that piece by Cyclops; if he had turned himself into a female Dinah Shore he still knew his business and could hold his own with the best in the needle trades. Let Farber be quick, he would be as quick. At least as quick. Oh, when the moment came he, he could strike a blow or two.

That moment, it is generally accepted, seemed close at hand when Farber slouched onstage to somewhat ambiguous applause. Considering Shane's introduction ("I want to bring out a guy who brings to mind memories of an older America, memories like smallpox, yellow fever and diphthe-ria; a guy who speaks out fearlessly on the issues of the day and is right now protesting the American presence in Miami Beach; a guy whose exchange with Groucho Marx is part of show business legend: 'Say, is that a Malibu exchange?' 'No, it's a Brentwood exchange.' . . .') Farber should have by all rights played rough beast and candy store Caliban. Perhaps, in fact, he had some such intention, for he first spoke his old harsh "Love me, love me, love me."

He said "Love me, love me, love me" and directed at the audience a look of dreamy curiosity.

He slightly humped his back and braced his shoulders and an expression of princely acquiescence crossed his face. *Like Lassie pulling at a trouser-leg,* I noted, *like some wonder horse pounding hoofs on a ranch house step he is trying to tell us something—but what, what, what!*

He began or seemed to begin well enough.

"Everybody has good taste; the world is dying of teakwood and butcher block."

But he had only beginnings.

"Darkness I love; what scares me are the power utilities."

And, "It costs us a fortune for orthodontia but our children's teeth are anyway set on edge."

And, "In my father's house there are many Mansons."

And, "The time is at hand when the wearing of prayer shawl and skullcap will not bar a man from the White House—unless, of course, the man is Jewish."

Then cries of "Get him!" and "Hold him!" rose sharply from the audience. I lost sight of Farber, and when I flicked a glance at the monitor I began to blink blindly, for I believed I beheld him levitate.

But it was only the sickening dip and swoop of the cameras as they tracked his lovely, looney topple from the stage. What matter that in his grief he knew what he was doing, that his repertoire of tumble tricks was nearly as extensive and exquisite as Dick Van Dyke's, that a pair of husky ushers rode out his impact with their hands? I make my own connections—to rites of passage, to dismembered gods, to heroes bearing mankind their dangerously won boons, to movie gangsters taking the benediction of bullets.

"People," he murmured, smiling fully and happily.

He murmured "People, people," saluting with the hand mike.

And prowling the aisles he commenced speaking up in his most powerful voice.

"My mother hit harder than your mother.

"We had a crazier girl on our block.

"My mother was more possessive than your mother.

"My mother cooked fattier foods than your mother.

"I stole more deposit bottles than you, sneaked into more

movies, wrote dirtier words on the blackboard, ate worse junk, got lower marks."

And mumblings.

And concussive sounds.

For someone's hand is waving in Farber's face, someone else's striking at the mike.

"—A question."

"—We have."

A young couple, jittering and flouncing in their aisle seats, address him.

"—curious about."

"—to know."

Both wear faces of soothing dumbness, like fresh-sliced meat.

"—we were on the 'Newlywed Game.' "

"—trying out for."

"—*before* the tryout, it was the *pre*-tryout, honey."

They rise, they sit, trying to smile at each other. Then only the wife rises.

"See," she says pleasantly, "their question was for the husband, the husband is an obscene caller—"

"An obscene telephone caller. Telephones, Mitzi!" The husband is on his feet.

Then there were giggles and desperate openmouthed kisses. And the wife, her tongue still flicking, went on to say, "You are an obscene *telephone* caller . . . if you were . . . say you were placing me this obscene telephone call you would say to me what?"

"I would say," Farber answered out of his grumpy silence, "you know what I would say? On me don't count!"

He sauntered off, stopped, seemed to peer into the far distance.

"A little louder," he cried.

Laughter, coarse and ribald, came from the balcony, then a ferment of strong falsetto voices.

"TODAY KING KONG WOULD HAVE BEEN SIXTY-EIGHT YEARS OLD!"

With pain in his eyes Farber said, "He's better off. Believe me, he's better off. If he lived he'd be stuck in New York, alone like a stone. And he'd end up—you know how he'd end up? Walking a Doberman pinscher with an interior decorator. 'Kingee, you know I cahn't stand it when you sulk, you're being beastly, you beast. What is it now, you gorgeous hussy? Really, we don't *have* to go to Ischia again. We can do the Hamptons, dear boy. Go ape on some peachy beachy. Because I'm dying to see you in that puce bikini. With those mah-ssive pectorals. . . .' "

A station break.

And when next seen Farber is dealing with a stack of cards.

Saying, "You filled these out on line, right? Am I right? Because I want to say you write very very clearly. You don't think clearly but you write clearly. See, that's one thing about my people—they don't write clear. Can you blame them? You shouldn't blame them; they learned handwriting on the back of brown paper bags."

A loving loutishness, by slow degrees, spread over his face.

"Who wrote this . . . this? Look, look at me, make believe you're reading a meter. *Are you easy to live with?* To live with yes, to be married to no. *I am curious to know where you get your material.* Usually from an unmarked truck. *Do you think Yiddish is more expressive than English?* Nah, it just seems that way on account of we have more to express. *How would you like to come back in a second life?* Any way, except by Delta Airlines. *What special kind of woman turns you on?*"

He closed one eye, then the other, like a nervous photographer.

Answering sweetly, shakily, "Bakery ladies."

He said, "Yeah yeah, bakery ladies," and put out an arm as if drawing the audience close. "I don't know why and I don't want to know, but . . . let them be ninety-three years old with a hump and cotton in the ears and a wandering eye and hair in the moles and orthopedic shoes and half-socks. . . .

Only the second they start doing that 'These are your prune Danishes and these are your fudge brownies and these are your German chocolate cakes' I get flashes and I whistle string quartets and I babble—do I know what I'm babbling? 'Tell me, can you tell me this: If you're on safari is it a good idea to freeze the sour rye? Want to grow some mandrake root? How about starting a new magazine? That Pentagon sure knows how to hurt a guy. . . .' "

He let the next one, two, three cards pass without comment.

Then he nodded and swayed.

"*Why was Israel hostile to McGovern's candidacy?*"

He squeezed his hands white.

"On account of the Wailing Wall," he answered.

"See," he picked up, "McGovern made this secret trip to Israel and they naturally wanted to show him around. 'What—what can we show you, Senator?' 'Well. . . .' He thinks and he thinks. 'Bases and factories are pretty much alike the world over. Perhaps . . . perhaps something of historical and religious significance to your young nation.' 'The Wailing Wall—how about the Wailing Wall?' 'The Wailing Wall will be grand.' So Golda herself takes him to the Wailing Wall. And she watches. And she waits. While he stands there ten minutes . . . fifteen minutes . . . an hour . . . an hour-and-a-half. He's back two hours later. 'Two hours at the Wailing Wall! Must have been for you some moving experience, Senator.' 'Oh, grand, grand,' he says. 'And will you invite me back again when I'm President?' 'Of course, with the greatest pleasure.' 'Because by then I imagine the entire building should be completed. . . .' "

He awaited laughs, settled for titters.

Then, "Devoted Admirer, let me see Devoted Admirer."

"From earliest days"—a meaty orange-headed woman leaned across two laps, blew kisses off all her ten fingers—"and from your original beginnings."

"Thank you, many thanks"—he appeared stirred, shaken—"because you're a really warm and wonderful person, and my earnest, my heartfelt hope is . . . in years to come . . . they should be able to deport you to Eastern Silesia."

"Because of your comic work"—she grabbed at his hand, slowly stroked her cheek with it—"we are brought to better insight over the very real problems we got today on the American scene."

"You look . . . you know how you look?" he amiably remarked. "Like you do funny things with cocktail franks."

"What has me concerned and maybe you have an answer . . . the education system *and* all the open frankness parents are doing—"

"You're trembling," he rushed in, "or you're wringing a rag?"

"—is there such a thing as, with today's American kids, and all you do is you talk to mine, that they know too much?"

Silence.

"They know too much," he said hotly. "America, you hear? Can you live from that, America? They know—you know what they know? Guitars. . . ."

Through his nose and all eight sinus cavities he twanged,

> *"If you were a carpenter*
> *And I was a paraplegic*
> *Would you fix my wagon?*
> *Would you fix my wagon?"*

He said, "God forbid—God forbid, ut-ut-ut and poo-poo-poo you should mention to a kid something that requires a fact. You ask him, 'Hey, your father, what does your father do? I mean, how does he, like, make a living?' They give you a look, your mother's milk freezes. 'Right now,' he answers, 'it's not on my reading list but I think, I'm not sure, I think we cover it next year in "Marriage and the Family." ' Later you find out the father's been dead five years. But what do you want from the kid? After all, he's only twenty-two and he hasn't . . . he hasn't yet . . . *absorbed* death.

He has to first get over the loss of his turtle. You see him, he's walking around with a mandarin beard and a copy of the *Kama Sutra,* and his mother's telling him, 'Don't be depressed over the turtle, Muffin, Muffin, you're depressed, maybe we'll get you some of the real stuff, the Tijuana grass, remember, Muffin, you shouldn't aggravate, you should be happy your turtle is in turtle heaven, he's sitting right next to the throne of the Great Turtle God.' Me. . . ."

He dwindled off.

He dwindled off but came back strongly, saying, "I think when I was seven-and-a-half I was already a cardiovascular specialist. 'You know what, Mom? Mom! I think with Cousin Izzy's history of circulatory disorders he should immediately be put on anticoagulants to avoid the possibility of phlebitis.' By the time I was ten I could have qualified for an advanced degree in mourning: I had already been to more cemeteries than Burke and Hare. 'Will you follow me, Mom! Mom, just follow me, we can save ourselves walking if we turn left at Row B and then straight ahead, straight by the Pincus plot.' And when we got to the grave and she started carrying on I would coach her. 'Mom, don't forget, you have to tell Grandpa how Dr. Nadelman did such a lousy job on your bridge, how it's three years and the gums are still bleeding. . . .' "

He moved off, but the woman's voice moved after, stopping him with a "Jules, could it partially be that they, the young people, kids are . . . they are suffering the lack of spiritual leadership from our rabbis?"

"I understand your question," he replied, "and I too share your concern. In fact I'm even more concerned because I can understand your question."

He opened and closed a palm.

He bounced an unseen ball.

"What do you, what does everybody want from the rabbis?

"Do you come to them anymore with real problems?

"When—when was the last time you said, 'Rabbi, I'm

a little bit worried, I'm a little bit anxious; my son had this argument with the Devil, now, all of a sudden, he dropped dead under the wedding canopy. I'm not only ashamed for the guests but we left a big guarantee with the caterer, so what do you say, Rabbi, huh, maybe you could bring him back to life, it's a pity for my Cousin Abe and his family, they made such a big trip in from Trenton, New Jersey. . . .'

"Do you ever ask him, 'Rabbi, when you have a little time, it doesn't have to be on the minute, could you maybe exorcise a dybbuk; I notice my daughter lately is growing hair behind and horns in front.' Or a practical question, something he's trained to handle? 'Rabbi, give me your judgment: Should I invest in municipal bonds or should I divide my fortune among the first seven beggars I meet along the road to New Rochelle?' "

His "Nah!" was still increasing in volume and intensity when someone from the balcony trilled, nastily trilled, "SEND ME A STAMPED SELF-ADDRESSED ENVELOPE AND I WILL SEND PROOF OF TARZAN'S JEWISH ORIGINS."

"People, people, save your stamps," Farber advised. "Because I got a little announcement. Tarzan . . . Tarzan," he croaked, "isn't Jewish. Cheetah is. I mean, what do you think he's talking all the time in Tarzan's ear? 'You big dumb clunk, you yutz, you, right ahvay I'll give such an ungraded moron minimum-wage scale, in your *shmutzy* loincloth I'll give you, you low-life. Tree houses I should build him also, be grateful you get hah basement in downtown Uganda, pay attention because right now on the instant second you're making delivery to Mrs. Schatzenberger, 5-G, that she called three times, she wants a case Hoffman's, mixed flavors, don't forget the empties, tzvelve empties you should bring back, *vei*, I needed this, I had to become an Equal Opportunity Employer. . . .' "

Then he flinched.

He flinched and gaped.

At a skinny young man with lank cheeks, a toothbrush mustache and skin the color of burnt coffee.

"Monsoon, monsoon," he cried, and "Famine," and "Khyber Pass."

"Yes sar."

"Can you use a pair of pajamas? A nice little beggar's bowl? Because you're from India, you're an Indian kid, right?"

"Yes sar."

"When you go back—and there's no rush; wait at least till you run out of curry—you'll say hello to Mrs. Gandhi. You know Mrs. Gandhi?"

"Yes sar."

"That's some woman. In your country—I bet in your country you don't see too many women like Mrs. Gandhi."

"Oh no sar."

"After all, she's not pregnant."

Station break.

"Back here, Julie. Here, you didn't go here yet."

And the camera moved in for a very close close-up of a blue and white El Al flight bag.

"Julie, Julie, we're from BROOKLYN!"

Pause.

". . . from Flatbush near Hawthorne."

"I'm dying, I'm dying." Farber socked his chest. "From Flatbush near Hawthorne. That means, it means you are, you have to be. . . ."

He chuckled softly, yearningly.

"You're right right near that . . . oh, it's there for years, that big, that huge appetizing store."

"Shimmel's, are you talking about Shimmel's?"

"I'm talking about Shimmel's. I want you to go into Shimmel's. . . ."

"I am there three and four times a week, *at least* three and four times a week."

"You should go in . . . you know when you should go in?

On a Thursday. Because on Thursday they get their ship-
ments of tainted shmaltz herring."

He drifted away, as though on a journey that would take
years, his hands leading lives of their own while he sang,

> *"Sixteen Jews in a cemetery plot*
> *Fifteen had adhesions and one had a clot. . . ."*

Then, "Mister. . . ."

He snapped, "Mister, you look so worried, you look so
anxious. Whaha you so worried, whaha you so anxious? They
started hirin' again at GE?"

An elderly sharp-faced man with rimless eyeglasses smiled
wanly, spoke a few words impossible to catch.

"Articulate, move the lips a little," Farber said. "Make
believe you're reading the newspaper."

"I AM NOT . . . Jewish."

"I knew when I looked at your wife," said Farber. "This
is your wife, right? Am I right? A real American beauty."

"No Jewish person in White House. . . . You said. . . . Fail
to see. . . . I. . . ."

"I like her outfit, her whole ensemble."

"Speak myself only. . . . He, if qualified. . . . No matter
religious belief. . . . Would not let. . . ."

"Smart, very smart the way the black pocketbook matches
the gums."

"For him my vote . . . regardless."

"Isn't he something!" Farber exclaimed. "It's people like
you"—he spread a palm over the gaunt head—"people like
you laid down the foundations of America so people like me
should have to pay a fortune for unfinished homes. Nah, nah,
I know you mean well, but when it comes to having a Jewish president forget it and never again."

Pause.

"Never again. I say 'Never again' because they had one
already and they had to hush it up. Oh, *he*—he was all right.
Only the wife. That wife, that wife! I mean . . . the Surgeon

General couldn't take it from her no more. Three times a night . . . 'Hello, Surgeon General, dear, I wondered if maybe you could get my brother-in-law a Walter Reed Hospital checkup, I know you should be what they call a veteran, he's not exactly a veteran but during the World War II conflict he specialized in uniform alteration only. . . .' Then on the NBC tour of the White House she kept complaining there wasn't enough closet space . . . The Attorney General she didn't even talk to . . . 'One little phone call he couldn't make for me, where he'd get a few bucks and I'd get a few bucks, I even had written down what he should say: Hello, Mr. Heinz, mine client bought a recent bottle your fine ketchup, the family size, on or upon opening same came jumping a cockroach of disgusting proportion causing her distressed mental anguish, we can settle without no lawyer letters, you carry after all a German name so I don't need define by you the word reparations. . . .' And the President—the poor guy would get into his helicopter, she'd start yelling from the window, 'It's on your way, what does it hurt, you mean-spirited person, drop my mother off by the BMT. . . .' "

For a short bitter time he went about laying on hands, saying, "I hope they steal your rubber cushion"; and "That's a vaccination mark or a Stop sign"; and "I hope your lamp bases turn back into Chianti bottles." But by a woman with the immense puffy powerful face of a cartoon bulldog he chose to linger.

"I'm paranoid," he announced, "but you're anyway my enemy."

Then, "I worry you? I cause you concern? Don't, ah don't be concerned and don't be worried. I mean, on account of me they won't make a pogrom. All right, they might hit you . . . but how long can they hit you? Because they wouldn't have the energy. Which is how we planned it. Yeah yeah, we planned it, we warned them, we even printed it on our shopping bags and with every half-pound halvah we gave it away. All right, maybe we went wrong with the title, the title was a little too Jewish. After all, *The Protocols of the Elders of Zion. . . .*"

As though raising a scepter he raised his mike.

Chanting, "Then spake Rabbi Israel: And the sages do say that we shall weaken their vitals, yea, with fish sticks and red hots shall we pierce their bowels. For hath He not promised us, blessed be His Name of Names, that He will send us an angel, and the angel will put them in confusion and alarm, for He shall cause their shelves to be empty of Campbell's Soups, and we shall fall upon them, yea, we shall smite them with the slats from our venetian blinds. . . ."

Then he cried, "People, people!"

He patted fannies in the air.

"Love me, love me, love me—and if your brother falls don't let him move until he first gets at least two witnesses."

Here ends the videotape.

I spent fifteen minutes waiting for him outside the make-up room, another five, perhaps, walking in and out of the washrooms, from each to each calling "Hi, guy," then "Nu, schmuck?" In one of these washrooms a stagehand found me, handed over a twenty dollar bill across which Farber had grease-penciled:

> *It's the human condition*
> *It's the sinus condition*
> *Anyway take a taxi*
> *P.S. We'll talk*
> *P.P.S. Come back with change*

I was angry and slept poorly most of that night, drifting off to *Mr. Muggs Goes to College*, awakening into a groggy recapitulation of childhood: The morning cartoons were on and Tom, with all his might, was chasing Jerry. At six-fifteen A.M., still debating between "At least you could have squeezed my tits," and "My mother can beat up your mother," I twice dialed Farber's number. There was no answer, though as it turns out Dr. Lubash was in the house. "This is me, that's how I am," he afterwards explained. "I can never pick up a phone when I'm filling out a death certificate."

5

At Least
It's a Jewish Word!

With Mrs. Lillian Federman
in the Park Slope Section of Brooklyn, New York

Chandler Van Horton's kindness is not forgotten.

This is your special message from Pop; I just hung up on him.

Yes, I told him you would be at Julie's unveiling and he cried and then I cried at how fast the time goes, that it should be a year already. Thank God that in the middle the bell rang; it was Essie, she was returning a sweater she borrowed to go down to the laundry room. Pop wanted to know who it was, I said it was Essie returning a sweater she borrowed to go down to the laundry room.

Well!

Or, as Essie says, '*Nu, nu, nu!*'

Because the minute I mention sweater he starts to laugh —Chandler, I have not heard Pop laugh like that since *The Honeymooners* when it was still a half-hour show. He

could only say "Chandler" and "sweater" and "Chandler
and his sweater."

Mom at that point had to grab the phone and she first
told me the whole story with you and your sweater, which I
gather has now made the rounds of the condominium and
the clubhouse.

Remember?

I bet you don't remember.

I'll give you a tiny hint, that it has to do with a certain
Jewish ritual or traditional custom concerning knives.

You know what . . . ?

Forget that hint, as I realize it could be slightly misleading.

I would instead say . . . oh, look at the sweater you had
under your jacket at the funeral, though knowing you and
how immaculate you are I wouldn't be surprised if you threw
it out.

See, I never noticed what had happened as from that point
I must have been conked out in the back of one of the
limousines. I had been okay, I had been fine and in good
control until . . . I started thinking of how for his bar mitzvah Julie wrote his own speech and from that I got pangs
because he wouldn't see Mitchell bar mitzvah. That plus an
empty stomach—which was a mistake since it turns out *all*
the airlines carry now special kosher cuisines upon request—
finished me off.

But I realize now why on the trip home Rabbi Bombawitz kept asking and asking me, "He's not Jewish?" and
"You know for a fact he's not Jewish?" and "He told you
definitely he's not Jewish?" I didn't take the question too
seriously, in fact I was quite annoyed with him through the
whole trip; Julie's body was still warm in the grave and he
couldn't wait to drop hints about how we're going to me-
morialize him and how his synagogue needs new benches,
his synagogue needs new fixtures. Personally I have very little
use for him; I'll be honest with you, Chandler, I don't feel
he did an especially outstanding grave-side officiating, or at
least not outstanding enough to justify the small fortune

we shelled out bringing him from East Flatbush. He happens, however, to be distant family, he has quite a reputation (he's a something on the New York Board of Rabbis), and he's Orthodox. This Orthodox factor really was the most important factor since my parents insisted and it was all on my shoulders. All right, probably that Jewish writer isn't altogether wrong, and "there are Jews everywhere," only let *him* go find an Orthodox rabbi in California.

Still, whatever my private opinion, the man is close to eighty with an impaired vision handicap. In fact, Mom claims that even without an impaired vision handicap he shouldn't be blamed for his mistake, that a person of 20/20 vision could make out a case for you being Jewish, and I must agree.

See, it wasn't only your beard, but you had right away gone over to Rabbi Bombawitz and said to him, "*Shalom,* sir." Oh, also you were handing out the yarmulke skullcaps to the men. All right, you don't need to be Jewish to have familiarity with our customs. Didn't I once have a girl who told me "I ain't doing for you"—this is her grammar—"next Friday, Mrs. Federman, you forgot next Friday is *erev Slichus.*" And most, naturally not all, but *most* gentiles come across under any conditions as gentiles. Take a Sargent Shriver. He spoke once at Mom and Pop's condominium and I understand the total sentiment was "that the more you feed him chicken fat the more he'd smell from bacon."

No, in my mind what clinched your Jewishness for Rabbi Bombawitz was that Buddy Hackett cried and Shecky Greene cried and Alan King cried and Don Rickles cried and Jackie Mason cried, but you *wept.* Also he must have noticed Mom was hugging you and telling everybody you were like a good brother to Julie, which is absolutely true, and he heard only the "brother." (It's a wonder to me he heard even that, the man was so busy trying to make an impression: Buddy Hackett told me Don Rickles at one point had to say, "I'm sorry, Rabbi, I only do a single.")

Now first I bet you remember!

Mom swears that when she saw him going for you with his little knife and making a cut in your sweater she wanted to yell, but she didn't yell for two reasons. First of all, you don't yell on a rabbi; secondly, she swears he was giving such a performance and making such a production she honestly was afraid he'd deal you a serious injury as those little knives can be very sharp. The whole custom, of course, is symbolic; you are symbolically rending or renting the clothes, though I could live a million years without the symbolism; I don't feel you should have to mourn somebody with knives. But thanks to Mom a little mystery is cleared up for me, as I never understood why when I asked you "What did you think of our Rabbi Bombawitz?" you answered me, "Well, he has some beautiful moves."

Oi!

I just noticed.

Essie gave me the wrong sweater.

Therefore she will be momentarily ringing the bell and when Essie walks in I'm finished for the night. Anyway, you wanted my reaction last time to those magazine articles and I started to tell you "Very nice." This was not right because I really hadn't read them, also they were borrowed by Essie who kept them and kept them. Anyway, I finally got through them—why do you call them *little* magazines? I only wish our *Young Israel Bulletin* could afford as many pages—and I am somewhat confused.

All right, it could be my own failings and lack of understanding. I remember in Brooklyn College getting a certain professor *whom* everybody wanted for "Aspects of Fiction"; he was so popular that two days before registration his class would be closed. As my luck would have it he calls upon me first thing, he had not even given out the reading list. Why, Miss Farber, Lillian, did the novel or the form of the novel appeal to the bourgeois middle class? My answer was that the novel provides a story and everybody is interested in a good story. Immediately he tore me down, which was how it was for the entire term; whether in my class discussions or my term themes I could never please him with a knowledge of social and economic stuff.

It's funny, but in the same way I felt torn down by these articles. First of all, if you're writing something about a person why don't you mention that person's name a few times? Because in both those articles you see one Jules Farber to ten and twelve mentions of Lenny Bruce and Woody Allen and Jonathan Swift and Leon Trotsky—where does Trotsky fit in?—and I think Father Berrigan. Also, if you're the author and the subject is a comedian does it hurt you to crack a little joke and to remind the reading public they should give all comedians a break? Believe me, a comedian doesn't have it so easy; take notice sometimes of Don Rickles, how the man gets wringing wet during a performance.

Certain things, I admit, hurt me personally in these articles, though these things could again be my own failings and lack of understanding. See, there's something Pop used to say when we were kids: You shouldn't look to find out from where your feet grow. In other words, if Julie was a good comedian let's be grateful for the few laughs he gave in his too-short lifetime. Don't start in with how he used to spit in the face of respectable culture and that he had dealings with the society the way the Katzenjammer Kids had dealings with the Captain; let people enjoy Julie, let people enjoy the Katzenjammer Kids.

Where I felt like writing in a letter, because that's how it got to me, was with this one professor—don't take insult!—with his business of Julie's broken heart; he continually has Julie's heart breaking from our blighted moral landscape or our morally blighted landscape. I wanted to tell him he shouldn't be such a landscape artist and if he's that interested in Julie's heartbreak I'll refer him to the one individual who absolutely and definitely and unquestionably deserves title as *the world's outstanding authority;* if they give out honorary degrees this one individual deserves to be a Doctor of Inhumane Letters.

Chandler, may I tell you something now?

I am now going to tell you something and I strongly have the feeling you already guessed my news.

Why do I have this feeling?

Because at the funeral when you were looking and looking and I asked you, "Chandler, what are you looking and looking for her, as I have not invited my former sister-in-law, Marlene Ungerer," you had a certain expression. Julie called this expression your "early-middle-Henry-Fonda-wiseguy-cornball expression"; he claimed, and I agree, that "nothing gets by Chandler except a check."

I had then figured that I might as well come across as the bad one; in other words let the world think I am showing my true prejudiced colors, my feelings now are out as to the low regard I always had for my non-Jewish sister-in-law but had to hide while my brother was still alive.

Well, I shouldn't live to answer the doorbell that Essie will any minute ring three times—it's our signal, that's what you have to do nowadays in our neighborhood—if I didn't call Marlene up; I called her before I even called Mom and Pop because the Florida circuits were as usual busy. "Marlene, my news will probably be of slight shock to you." "Most news, Lil, in the contemporary present is of shock to me." "Marlene, Julie is dead, he passed away." "Uh-huh, well which is it, Lil?" "The funeral is tomorrow, we'll naturally expect you, should we expect you, Marlene?" "Thank you very much, Lil, however I really am not actually interested."

This is what she said and this is how she stayed; the girl *would . . . not . . . budge*! I had to tell Mom and Pop a crazy lie, that in her religion there is a rule that when a couple is divorcing they can't go to each other's funeral. If they really believed me I wonder, as Mom said that when Robert Taylor died, he should rest in peace, Barbara Stanwyck who also is not Jewish—did you know she went to Julie's high school?—and was for years and years divorced from Robert Taylor went to the funeral. Of course, in one way I should be very grateful Marlene didn't come because

I'm afraid I couldn't have held myself from making a little scene. All right, in the actual situation and in front of all those people, many of whom, like yourself, Chandler, hold Jewish outlooks but still are not Jewish, I see myself most likely restraining ninety-nine percent of my total feelings. If you're interested, though, I can sometime mail you the little speech I wrote out for the occasion; it'll show how I cut down my opening remarks from "You're a murderer" to "You're guilty of willful homicide" to "You didn't do Julie any good."

I think you'll believe me, Chandler, if I swear to you I wish Marlene no harm. This is the mother of my nephew and what would hurt her would end up only hurting him. If I said, "Chandler, she killed him," you would have a right to answer, "Lillian, don't be a fool," and you'd bring out that Dr. Lubash said Julie had arteries like a sixty-five-year-old man.

So what?

Sixty-five-year-old men live on to be eighty-five- and ninety-year-old men and we could've had Julie with us for a nice long time, at least a little while yet if she had shown him even the slightest feeling.

Maybe it'll come back to you, Chandler, that when you drove us back to the airport—and please forget about picking us up for the unveiling, I won't even tell you when the planes get in: What are you, a shuttle?—I started to hint of this. I said, "Well, she did him in" or "Well, she finished her job."

You answered me with a Hemingway line, I think you told me Hemingway: "Lillian, life is a dirty trick." I then said "Life is a dirty trick and life is a dirty sink, she still fixed him up."

See if you'll remember your exact words. . . .

Remember?

"Lillian, a shikse is a shikse."

I gave you a kiss, that's how cute it struck me at the time. Only what did I answer?

I said, *"Chandler, a shikse is a shikse but also a Jew is a Jew."*

You looked at me as if to say, "Lillian, I hope you will enlarge upon your last remark," and I looked at you as if to say "Chandler, we're both better off if I don't enlarge upon my last remark because these involve matters which have to be brought out at the right time and in the right way."

Now probably—and I shouldn't say "probably," knowing you—your knowledge of Jewish history would reveal me as the real dope I am. How many times do I catch myself saying Palestine instead of Israel? And if I picked up a Jewish newspaper I wouldn't be able to read it, this is after between four and five years of Talmud Torah education.

So do not, please, for one moment interpret what I have to say in the wrong light—in other words that because you weren't Jewish, Julie didn't give you his fullest confidence.

But there are certain things only a Jewish person can understand, which is why I say again, Chandler, *a Jew is a Jew.*

Let him go to a temple, let him not go to a temple, let him eat the worst non-kosher junk, let him fast on Yom Kippur, let him gorge on Yom Kippur, let him be ashamed of his name, let him be ashamed of his nose, let him give a penny, let him give a dollar, let him not even give to our institutions, let him marry a Marlene—and still, Chandler, *a Jew is a Jew.*

There are all kinds of Jews, naturally, only usually, notice my usually, when it comes to a certain issue there is *usually* just one kind of Jew.

This issue is conversion.

Now I'm positive, Chandler, that if you intermarried and had a Jewish wife and one day she *discussed* with you the idea of converting the children to Judaism you would very possibly go for the idea, or if you didn't go for it you wouldn't take the matter to heart.

So why a Julie who had gotten so far away from Jewishness should take it to heart if Marlene wanted to convert Mitchell probably makes no common sense to you. Unfortunately, and it is unfortunate, common sense has nothing to do with it.

After all, you could say if we had common sense we wouldn't be Jewish. Because if you applied logic, if you asked the average Jew whether Christ wasn't a wonderful person, definitely one of the most wonderful people in history, he would have to answer Yes, and that Christ deserves all the respect he gets. Now an Essie is just such an average Jew; we have on occasion discussed the question, and she admits Christ was one of the most wonderful people in history. She, however, makes the point that Eisenhower could also be considered a wonderful person, but that doesn't mean she's willing to join the Republican Party.

This is how Essie is, this is to a certain extent how we all are; as I say, it has nothing to do with logic and common sense and the fact that in every way other religions have their own beauty of custom and ritual. Some years ago, for instance, I had to return something to Best & Co., this is when Best & Co. still was in business, and I happened that day to go near St. Patrick's Cathedral. I must tell you I looked inside and I got jealous, not only because it is an absolutely gorgeous building, our Temple Emanu-El takes an easy back seat, but because the people as they went in had a certain look of real pleasure. They were crossing themselves and they were kneeling and they were lighting candles and they were enjoying their little observances. Here, I would say, is where we don't compare favorably, because while the Jewish religion has probably as many enjoyable observances I don't feel Jews enjoy them as much.

Anyway, I'm sure there are arguments that could be made for both sides, and though I still think a Jew is a Jew I also think it's wonderful, or at least it certainly doesn't hurt to have rabbis and priests together without nastiness on things like the "David Susskind Show" or joining in matters of mutual interest under the sponsoring of human relations agencies. As far as Marlene is concerned I cannot take away from her the privilege of wanting to convert Mitchell; where I have it in for her is that in the process she resorted to real nastiness.

Now I have seen in at least two similar cases of inter-marriage how the couples went for marriage counseling and ended up with the Unitarians. Couldn't Marlene have done something like that? And if she didn't like the Unitarians there are also the Quakers and the Ethical Culture groups; in this way Mitchell would have been definitely not Jewish but also not exactly a Christian.

All right, she didn't want that. She wanted her special variety of church, a church nobody heard of; the big estab-lished ones weren't good enough for her. Therefore to a great extent, Chandler, I blame her actions on that church because the big established ones teach you nowadays to be-have with a little dignity, decency and democracy. And why not? Do they need us so badly in the fold? I several times over the year have been on the verge of calling her Christ Therapist people with that question, whether they're so hard up for converts as to have their followers act along the lines of Marlene.

You know what stopped me?

I frankly was afraid they would answer me "Absolutely not, lady," and "Lady, we disclaim all responsibility."

Why was I afraid?

Because this would mean Marlene acted on her own and that my original judgment of her was so altogether off.

See, to me, Chandler, she was a pleasant, good-natured girl who definitely didn't fit into any stereotype; when she came into the family you would never have said a *shikse* is a *shikse* in the sense that she was . . . oh, reserved; many Jews feel all non-Jewish girls are reserved or withdrawn. Mom is typical, and I would always point out to her that the reason is we encounter non-Jewish girls mostly through their occu-pations. They are bank tellers or checkout girls or they work for the phone company where you're not allowed to be out-going. On the contrary, Marlene as I got to know her proved extremely outgoing and extremely natural and extremely lively. And let me assure you, Chandler, I got to know her; the way I got to know Essie is the way I got to know Marlene. We went shopping together; I mean really shopping, day in and day out shopping, from store to store shopping, furniture and carpeting shopping. And tell me, please, how much more intimate can you be with a person than when you help organize their closets?

Well, I hope to God I had her wrong. I want to be the world's biggest dumbbell. If not, if she is your normal average non-Jewish *shikse* girl then Jews should stop fooling themselves, because that's what they're doing with the Anti-Defamation League and similar organizations which go around telling you prejudice is a sickness, prejudice is a disease. Maybe Julie was right in his attitude to them; he used to say, "Hey, the biggest, the strongest, the healthiest ox just called me Jew-bastard."

No, oh no, Chandler, rest assured Marlene never used these or similar terms on Julie. However, don't consider me crazy if I say I wish she had. Oh, I'm sure it would have given him suffering, it would have been painful to him, but he would have been better off; I mean better off in the way that a person with a kidney stone is better off than a person with cancer.

Anyway, I'll tell you what gets me.

Shall I tell you what gets me, Chandler?

That when Marlene started her actions I was delighted; it shows you how ingenuous or disingenuous I am as a judge of human character.

See, the house was filled with my Young Israel girls, and when the phone rang it interrupted the reading of the minutes, also this was when Tony the super picked to come and fix the toilet, he kept flushing and flushing it in my ear. Between that noise and the noise the girls made, God bless them. . . .

I therefore understood Julie to say only that he'd come across a pamphlet, that it was Marlene's pamphlet, the pamphlet had something to do with circumcision—*How Circum-cision Weakens* or *Weakening by Circumcision.*

And to me this was good news.

I even said to Julie, "Julie, you know what? To me this is good news."

He started saying "Revenge" and I answered "Julie, it's reconciliation; Marlene obviously is looking to reconcile with you. Poor kid, she's trying to show you that she's taking an interest in the customs and traditions of Judaism."

Till he called the next time this is what I thought, in fact I was on the verge of mentioning something to Essie; thank God I never had the chance, she went on jury duty and right from jury duty to the hospital for polyp removal. Whether he said, "She did it again" or "She's done it again" I don't remember. *I* thought it was something with his house-keeper; he constantly claimed she was breaking all his major appliances. This happens with some girls, though it's not necessarily their fault. Years ago I had one, she'd give such a yank on the toaster handle your mezuzah could fly off the door.

Well, he started reading to me, for a while I found it interesting. It was about Albert or Alfred Dreyfus and Ethel and Julius Rosenberg and Louis Brandeis and Felix Frank-furter. Then Julie told me the title; the title was *Great Jewish Traitors.* "Julie, where did you get it?" "Where did I get it? It's the script for the new "Jerry Lewis Special"; it's the *Reader's Digest* version of *Herzog;* it's the special book bonus if you subscribe to the Syracuse *Pennysaver. . . .*" "Seriously, tell me seriously, Julie, where did you get it?"

It was in Mitchell's little visitation day suitcase, and Julie noticed it immediately because the suitcase was clean.

Now to tell you what happened next, Chandler, I have to go back . . . I would say close to a hundred years. Easily a hundred years. This is family legend; in other words our family has a legend. See, my grandfather Lazar Wolf, which in English would be, oh, Billy Lou, is supposed to have been *extremely* religious; he was so religious and also such a nice person, the two don't necessarily go together, I don't have to tell you, Chandler, that they called him the *zaddik*, which is like a Jewish saint.

In fact, they tell a story about how religious he was, the story is that my grandmother came home from a long long trip, she'd been away maybe a year, and she returned home just in time for Yom Kippur. My grandfather meets her, and with him are the children; they had, I honestly don't know whether eleven or twelve children. Well, something, something is bothering her. She wants to know if anybody is missing; "Who's missing?" My grandfather tells her nobody is missing, her brains are missing, and during those years, particularly amongst Jews, though not only Jews, the husband is king and she takes his word. Also there's a lot to do for Yom Kippur, you can imagine how they observed Yom Kippur, and she's kept very very busy. So everybody gets dressed up, everybody goes to synagogue *and* finally the shofar ram's horn is blown *and* finally it's sundown *and* finally they sit down to their meal *and* finally they finish up *and* finally everybody goes to bed. "You know what," my grandfather says. "I want to tell you something. I kept it back and I held it in, but you were right and somebody is missing; our little"—I'll make up a name, I'll say Chaneleh—"our little Chaneleh is missing." See, over that year my grandmother was gone one of her daughters had died of . . . I'll say cholera, because during those years they used to die a great deal of cholera. And my grandfather was such a saintly *zaddik*, so highly religious an individual that he kept the tragic news back from my grandmother lest it interfere with their celebration—I should say, really, observance—of Yom Kippur. It shows you, Chandler, not only his religious zeal but the holy significance of Yom Kippur. Absolutely nothing is allowed to interfere with it, to the extent that should a person die *in the synagogue*, I believe this happened with a friend of Pop's, the person's body has to stay where it is and cannot be touched until Yom Kippur is over.

Now my grandfather had a prayer shawl; this is known to

us as a *talith*. The most gorgeous thing! Because today the art of making *talithes* or *talithem* is practically a lost art, and that *talith* was a work of art. This gorgeous *talith* with its rich tradition of old country handicraft my grandfather gave to Pop or maybe Pop took it when he died, that's not important. But Pop gave it to Julie on the occasion of his bar mitzvah confirmation and Julie wore it when he took his picture. I'll never forget how the photographer said "I'm jealous of that *talith*, that *talith* is a knockout"; what's cute is that the photographer wasn't even Jewish.

Well as far as Julie knew he still had it, though it turns out it must have been mixed in with Mitchell's things which Marlene packed when they separated; I can imagine how she packed, as the girl is highly disorganized. It used to kill me the way she came back from shopping, she used to spend an hour and two hours putting away the cans by color: Del Monte green, then S&W green, then Palmolive Soap green. I used to plead with her, "Marlene, perishables first, perishables first. . . ."

Anyway, Marlene calls Julie. It's Halloween and he has to do a special favor for her because due to illness she can't go trick or treating with Mitchell. There's nobody else she can ask and even if she could ask she doesn't want to; after all, the little fellow has . . . special problems.

Why not?

Absolutely.

Fine.

He goes, he gets there, and Mitchell is waiting for him outside in the cutest little costume; he's dressed to be an Arab shepherd or sheepherder.

Only for a robe he's wearing . . .

You know what he's wearing for a robe?

Not only is he wearing my grandfather's *talith*, which is offensive and sacrilegious enough—see, Chandler, a *talith* is considered *a most holy object*; you could consider it like your crucifix; you wouldn't use your crucifix to hammer in a nail—but there are armholes cut into it and the collar or yoke is missing, this is all artisan handicraft, and most, not all but most of the fringes are missing; these are not merely fringes for the sake of decoration, Chandler, each fringe has a religious significance.

And you know what?

Chandler, I even then gave her the benefit of the doubt, I told Julie, "Look, it's annoying and it's aggravating but you have to realize the girl does not know any better, the girl comes from a background wherein she did not even know what a candy store was."

In fact, when she sent him a little program from her Christ Therapy people because Mitchell was going to be in their pageant or passion play—he had only a small part, I think he was like Cruel Rabbi Three—I gave Julie an argument. "Listen, kid brother, you forget but I remember how you pestered Pop to take you to Radio City for the Christmas Show; you're manifesting attitudes of prejudice; you're like Essie; her Heshie came home from kindergarten with a little drawing, she ran to the school and landed on the poor teacher because the teacher had taught that for stars you can make little crosses."

Anyway, what was important to me, Chandler, was that Mitchell was showing an improvement.

See, Marlene would dial Julie's number, she'd put on Mitchell and she'd get on the extension. "Mitch, how do Jewish people or peoples pray; Mitch, what do Jewish people or peoples say when they're laughing and what do they say when they're crying; Mitch, when Jewish people or peoples go to sleep and when Jewish people or peoples wake up they say—what do they say?" And the little fellow would go, "*Oi oi oi.*"

But he was verbalizing.

I'd tell him, "Julie, he's verbalizing, he's making comprehensible sounds."

Or I'd say, "Julie, let Marlene manifest bad taste and let Mitchell manifest his improvement."

Or I'd say, "Julie, at least he's coming out with a Yiddish word."

This, I think, was for two weeks.

One day she'd have Mitchell do the "*Oi oi oi*," another day a little duet with her. She would sing—you'll have to excuse me, Chandler if I sound like the song goes slightly against my grain; it's like if you had to sing, oh, "Mein Yiddishe Momma," I imagine it would also go slightly against your grain. . . .

> *He is my perfection*
> *He is my resurrection*
> *Oh how He giveth*
> *In Him I liveth*

Then there was something in Latin and right after the Latin Mitchell would join in: My Jesus, Jesus mine, My Jesus be. I heard how he does it, God bless him, the reason I heard it is because Marlene mailed me a little record; it was one of the things Mitchell did in his pageant or passion play; I'm afraid he inherited his aunt's voice.

And I would tell Julie, "Look, the kid is only having a good time in his theatricals, he's deriving pleasure, it's building up his ego and you should be in favor of anything from which he derives ego-building pleasure."

And I would tell Julie, "Good for you, see, you laughed at me when I wanted to have the kid for a few days, I wanted to put a little Jewish content in his life, he could have gone with me to a nice Yiddish musical on Second Avenue, at the time I wanted him I had tickets for *Kibbutznick from Brooklyn*."

And I would tell Julie, "Good for you, this is what you get, kid brother, I warned you and warned you, when it comes to a child's religion steps must be taken because God abhors a religious vacuum, you're giving the kid ninety-nine percent Christmas and one percent Chanukah, you're working him a beautiful identity crisis."

And I would tell Julie, "I wouldn't mind if I alone had warned you, but Pop said the same thing and Mom said the same thing and Aunt Pearlie said the same thing and Essie many times dropped a remark. What should we do if you wouldn't listen; you wouldn't realize that sometimes people don't mean harm. . . ."

Chandler, the time came when finally even I ran out of pleasantries.

One night, a Thursday, a week before he died, it had to be a Thursday because I was all set to go hear Elie Wiesel at Brooklyn College, this was part of their Thursday Night series, I hear from the hall, "Help, help, Lefkowitz, 2-F, they're killing mine wife!" "Hello, hello, Marcus, 3-L, is that two-and-a-half rooms, my sister's looking and looking!"

Naturally I recognized Julie's voice, also there's no Lefkowitz in the building.

"Lily, make me a *tzimmis*. . . ."

He gives me one carrot and one sweet potato; these, Chandler, are the basic *tzimmis* ingredients, though if you want a *good tzimmis* you have to add meat and let it cook . . . oh, for hours.

Then it hits me that he didn't come for *tzimmis*.

"Julie, you didn't come for *tzimmis*."

He puts his arms around me and he says, "I have got a smart sister" or "Have I got a smart sister!"

I told him, "You're a Julie-boolie funnyface" and "It's a funnyface boy" and "It's a face the sister has to love because it's a face not even a mother could love on payday"; see, this is how we talked to each other; for an older brother and a younger sister we were very close, extremely close.

And even if we weren't so close I would have known something was wrong.

You know how?

He didn't want chocolate milk.

Usually he went right to the refrigerator and took it himself and poured it into a certain glass, I used to call it the Julie glass.

Therefore I asked him directly and frankly and openly, "Julie, is anything of significance developing in regards to your situation?"

No, he wanted to come in to help celebrate the birthday of Daniel Boone Jefferson, this was the first black man to sing "Hava Nagila" at Grossinger's.

And he goes into the living room and he picks up a pepper mill and he starts swinging the pepper mill against my Venetian glass chandelier, this is a chandelier with thirty-five crystals, each crystal is almost thirty-five dollars to replace.

I tell him, "Julie, you know you're swinging that pepper mill against my Venetian glass chandelier, each crystal is almost thirty-five dollars to replace."

Chandler, I have heard the expression "a small voice"; a small voice is the only way to describe how he spoke; believe me, Chandler, if I say he spoke in a small voice.

"Marlene . . . release . . . with releases . . . she needed releases."

I said to him, "Julie, I wonder if in things like that husband and wife wouldn't be better off looking at it the way Max Lerner looks at it, that somehow we are all responsible."

This is when he broke two of my crystals.

"Press releases, Lily."

Goodbye one crystal.

"She sent out press releases."

Goodbye the other crystal and the Wedgewood sugar bowl; this bowl, Chandler, had survived three moves and three different furniture vans.

You know what kind of press releases?

That the son of a well-known Jewish-American or American-Jewish comic will be enjoying healing happiness in the arms of Christ Therapist; that the Brooklyn-born father has become noted for his many years of exposing the moral and ethical inadequacy of his people or peoples; that members of the press and photographers are cordially invited to coverage of the informal conversion ceremony.

Chandler, she sent them out all over.

In fact the only one she didn't send it to was Charles Stone, maybe you know his little column, he called up Julie to ask, "How come I'm the only one she didn't send it to?" Thank God nobody used it, I think because *Time* and *Newsweek* checked first with the American Jewish Congress or the American Jewish Committee and heard that in general the Christ Therapist group is not a group that inculcates healthily democratic attitudes.

I told him, "See, Julie, you have hitherto never considered our human relations agencies in any way save a negative way; I would love to see you from now on getting somewhat involved with them; if Theodore Bikel is involved with the Anti-Defamation League *and* Oscar Brand is involved with the American Jewish Congress *and* Pete Seeger is involved with the American Jewish Committee *and* Dore Schary is involved with all of them you likewise should consider—oh, not their kind of involvement but at least an active interest in some of their ongoing programs; certainly amongst their ongoing programs you could find a few in which to take an active interest; they are not perfect and who ever said they are perfect; they have nevertheless earned themselves respect for their role as shield, as public relations defense arm to the Jewish community. . . ."

This is when he put the scuff marks on my couch.

And this is when he tears out the little buttons of my Mexican tooled-leather hassock.

When he's finished tearing out the little buttons on my Mexican tooled-leather hassock he starts throwing around pieces of Barton's Dutch Delight with the liquid centers; they landed all over my windows and my walls; I had no trouble washing off the windows but one wall I had to cover with vinylized wall paper, I planned to do it anyway.

"*I'm going, Lily.*"

"Julie, this is no visit, Julie this is a flying visit."

"*Lily, Lily. . . .*"

"Should I try to make you a quick *tzimmis*?"

"Lily, Lily, Lily. . . ."

"Meatless *tzimmis* is also tasty."

"Lily, I'm a three-sewer hitter in a two-sewer world."

I went down with him to the street, Chandler, I stood with him until he got a taxi—we had to walk to Flatbush Avenue and then first three taximen heard Kennedy Airport, they raced away; the fourth one recognized Julie and did him a big favor, he charged him only twenty-three dollars.

Mom and Pope spoke to him one more time; they wanted to tell him Allie Shuman, he was an old friend of Julie's, turned out to be working for a big optical place on Collins Avenue and made up a pair of prescription sunglasses for Mom. I never got to speak to him again.

But you know what?

I heard from Marlene.

It must have been right after my *shiva* mourning because during the *shiva* mourning I wasn't opening mail; some say you're allowed but I like to play it safe. She sent me maybe forty little photos, the kind that is almost but not quite wallet-size, unless you have a tiny wallet; they showed Mitchell in the various stages of his conversion ceremony.

And I cried.

The image of Julie.

Julie number two.

I picked out a few, Chandler, I wanted enlargements made, but they explained to me that by the time you airbrush out—they have to use something called an airbrush—by the time they would airbrush out the crucifixes *and* by the time they would airbrush out the Virgin Mary *and* by the time they would airbrush out Marlene I would have practically nothing left. . . .

6

America and Other Sorrows

In assembling these interviews from some eight months of tapings my first concern was to present Farber's words exactly as he spoke them. I have rewritten nothing and have chosen to emphasize only what Farber himself emphasized, though in a few, a very few instances I have taken it upon myself to exclude passages given over rather too exclusively to the business of show business—i.e., Farber's relations with his agent, Carlotta D'Annunzio—or to Farber's lengthy, laborious litigations against (1) the National Bureau of Community Relations; and (2) its West Coast Director, Armand J. Rosenblatt. I would, however, cite for further reading Mr. Rosenblatt's own well-documented and dispassionate chronicle of these events in *The Jewish Community Relations Consultant*, Vol. 17, number 3 ("Ethnicity and the Ethnic Comic").

Finally, my particular thanks on this whole undertaking are due Miss Wendy Boynes, not only for her superb secretarial skills but for her willingness to absorb the subtle semantics of a life-style as different from her own as a milk shake is different from a malted.

VAN HORTON I understand from various of my colleagues that in 1969 you began declining all invitations, however high the honorarium, to appear before academic groups, that your replies, by postcard, were at best unkind, at worst hostile. Here on my clipboard are two which are not exactly exceptional: *I'd rather be buried in Queens* and *Get buried in Queens.*

FARBER It was academic lives and academic wives.

Also the deans.

The deans were always trying to relax me. . . .

"Say, did you ever read Marianne Moore on 'Major Herbs of the Northeastern Atlantic States'? She's also from Brooklyn. And may I say, incidentally, that I've never caught you on television . . . ?"

Then . . . then he hums a little "Cohen on the Telephone," he pours me a little Duff Cooper sherry, · the bottle has sediment from the Paleolithic Age, and he introduces me to the artist-in-residence. "We were terribly lucky to get him; he used to shingle roofs and shuck clams with Jackson Pollack during Pollack's roof-shingling clam-shucking period." And the artist is giving me looks—out of Gurdjieff by way of Madame Blavatsky. "Sunrise . . . shit-fuck . . . tree . . . cocksucker-prick . . . waterfall . . . cunt-snatch." He finds out I'm not a collector, he takes off; after all, why should he waste his charm?

And meanwhile. . . .

Meanwhile I'm trying, I'm dying to reach the food— three saltines and one mashed-up sardine. But a wife is pulling on me. And they're strong; academic wives are all strong. Because they do a lot of sanding, they sand down everything. "Brandeis! Do you know anyone at Brandeis? Kosher-kosher. Yeshiva U. Matzo-matzo. Appalachia? Sheepshead Bay? The Dust Bowl? Anywhere!" She has to get out of here because all the other faculty wives resent her, they're jealous of her wardrobe: Two babushkas with matching Ace bandages. Also her husband got this letter from the president: "Your work is totally unsatisfactory, your conduct unprofessional, your morals scandalous and you may be assured that under no circumstances will your contract be renewed for the next academic year." And if there's one thing she can't stand it's an equivocating administration.

Let me eat. . . .

She won't let me eat.

"Oh, save your appetite for Casa Wong-Wong, it's the finest of Chinese cuisine, the Modern Language Association always eats there."

Casa Wong-Wong is three blocks away but it's two hours of driving because they want to go by the scenic route. Which takes in an automobile graveyard, a kielbasa factory, a Dairy Queen, two compost heaps and a Rexall's with an exhibition of septic tank sculpture.

We get to Casa Wong-Wong and everybody is telling me, "Let Mr. Wong-Wong pick out the dishes, have confidence in Mr. Wong-Wong, he'll recommend from his special menu, his unlisted menu, Ralph Nader put us onto this place. . . ."

So Mr. Wong-Wong comes over. Mandarin beard, Anna May Wong robe, smelling from secret spices and clapping with one hand. "We're leaving it to you, Mr. Wong-Wong, Mr. Wong-Wong you're carrying the old ball, by George, in an age of declining standards we've never yet been disappointed by your suggestions. . . ."

He starts suggesting. . . .

"Mr. Wong-Wong humbly suggest dice flower yak broth, sifted walnut in happiness water, seven precious mushroom pudding, Peking Dust snowball and for dessert mixed plate spun-sugar noodle with green virgin bamboo bliss."

Everybody confers and everybody caucuses and they give the order: sub-gum cheeseburgers all around, a large

Dr. Pepper, vanilla ice cream and please bring chopsticks. The check is four ninety-seven, with tip that's five-and-a-quarter. A big argument. Who should sign for it? The dean signs. Oh, drat, he needs nine copies for the academic senate and say there, Mr. Wong-Wong, as long as you're going back for those copies perhaps a box of litchi nuts would be in order and, by George, take a look through the kitchen, see if you can spare a chunk of aromatic tea wood. . . .

Then—it's five minutes to showtime and they remember.

You know what they remember?

"Oh, chuckle-chuckle, you didn't know, Mr. Farber. A slight change of plans; you see that library cubicle is unavailable for your performance. . . ."

And we arrive at the amphitheater.

This amphitheater is the size of . . . I think it takes up the whole thirty-eighth parallel. And it's behind a drive-in showing *Tora! Tora!* and alongside an armory where they're holding mortar practice. Which is when the dean says to me, "By George, I certainly hope you don't have to work with a microphone."

VAN HORTON It seems to me you're saying, with Wilfred Sheed, that academics do everything badly.

FARBER They raise good hamsters. Lousy kids but good hamsters.

VAN HORTON I have the feeling that . . . Oh, no names, no names, but my impression is of a certain smallish progressive college founded in 1968 on the very highest of hopes. Hopes, I might add, which despite substantial funding . . . One would reach it by . . . To get there . . .

FARBER Let it be in . . . Poughkeepsie.

VAN HORTON Poughkeepsie?

FARBER Everywhere is Poughkeepsie. Where they call sour cream soured cream and make you pay fifteen cents extra. With a cute general store, and this general store has signs: *Canadian Money Will Be Discounted; We*

Belong to the Church of Manufacturer's Suggested Retail Price. With a cute little owner, and this owner tells jokes: "What would yuh be gettin' when yuh join a big box to a small chest? Women's Lib . . . !" And very law-abiding; a school bus stops, they stop—two states away. One TV channel—but it gets the Bowery Boys festival. One radio station—the station alternates between · Walter Brennan records and . . . news. News? I don't want to hurt your feelings, only how do you live from your news?

VAN HORTON My news?

FARBER Your news. Because my news is happy news, my news is Jewish news.

VAN HORTON Hannah Arendt will be pleased.

FARBER Don't you know—and keep up the whimsy; I'll throw you out with my old *New Yorker's*—you don't know that when you hear Jewish news you have to feel happy. All right, we have Hamans, we have holocausts. And once in a while we'll hear how an East New York *bubbee* is gang-banged . . . or Moey the pretzel-man is felled in a subway fire . . . or there's a bomb scare plus demands for racially balanced classes in a Hebrew school. . . .

But out there . . . in the Poughkeepsies . . . listen to your news, learn and find out what you go through.

A two-car collision at the Beidecke traffic circle has sent a West Wantago housewife to Shagmont Hospital with lacerations and possible internal injuries. According to Sheriff Ray Cashee, who headed the investigation, Mrs. Olga May Getch, 23, lost control of her small foreign car while attempting to pass a stake truck driven by Lyle Hubley, 79, a driver employed by the Non-Union Baking Company . . . An effort to thaw a frozen gas line has cost the life of a fifty-one-year-old White River resident, Floyd Bushing. A preliminary report made public today by Fire Chief Roy Grommet offers the theory that faulty wiring in the electric heater Mr. Bushing was using under his car may have caused the flash fire . . . A seven-year-old boy sustained spinal injuries today when he was struck by the family car in his own driveway. According to witnesses the boy, Ward Caulker, Jr., unexpectedly darted under the wheels of the vehicle driven by his mother, Mrs. Polly Caulker. Only last week Ward's sister, Billie Jo, 10, received neck and facial injuries when the brakes of her school bus failed to hold . . . And this just in: A broasted chicken supper, originally set for tonight by the VFW Post of Eagleton Village has been canceled in tribute to the memory of its commander, Lyle Wahlquist. Mr. Wahlquist, 55, died this morning at St. Thomas Hospital after contracting pellagra. . . .

VAN HORTON Is this, then, your point? That the sufferings of Jews are different from and deeper than the sufferings of all others?

FARBER Not different, not deeper. I would say . . . here's what I'd say: You *goyim* don't, simply don't know how to suffer. Am I blaming you? How can I blame you? It's a question of basic training. Your God, *He* feels for you, *He's* all the time suffering for you. Our God, you tell Him "It hurts, it hurts!" He'll answer "I know, I know, and in a minute you're going to hear me with some yell!"

VAN HORTON I'm reminded at the moment of Wyndham Lewis's lovely line—oh, let me not say "lovely"; let me say, rather, insightful. "Americans," he at any rate observed, "get very easily tired of their emotions."

FARBER He's right, and if I had their emotions I'd also get tired of them.

No, seriously . . . I'll be serious.

I'm jealous; that's the kiss-a-pinkie truth.

When I was fifteen I started getting jealous.

In a *goyisher* cemetery. Near Ferndale.

It had to be either a July Fourth or a Memorial Day. And I'm with a bucket on the Mohican Lodge driving range; I'm picking up balls. Where the two-hundred-yard line is there are bushes, and these bushes are right on top of the cemetery. A problem. Because if I'm going for the record—the record is ninety-six balls—I have to go into the cemetery.

But through the cemetery gates—a car.

Out of *The Grapes of Wrath*.

And the car stops by a little headstone: Verlin something, 1924–1944, died in Battle of Bulge, In Thy Nation's Memory Be Forever Enshrined, Beloved Son.

And a couple comes out . . . I couldn't stop looking at them. If you have a very good friend and your very good friend has parents these parents should live to look like this couple; in the movies they'd be Harry Carey and Fay Bainter.

Then three boy scouts.

One with a bugle and two with guns.

They fire a couple of volleys, one of the volleys is a misfire, they blow a little "Taps," the couple makes a salute, after the salute they put a fresh little flag on the headstone, and that's it.

That's it?

That's it.

This was a reaction?

This was a reaction.

Oh wowee.

I got so jealous.

I got jealous the way Boris Tomashefsky might have gotten jealous of Gary Cooper.

Should I tell you something else? I'm even jealous of your floods.

VAN HORTON Jung—I suspect it was Jung—makes somewhere the point that each race covets, unconsciously covets the disasters suffered by other races.

FARBER Oh, I enjoy your forest fires, I love a nice blizzard, a dry spell is also good, that's if you people don't overdo it with the parched earth and the *kvetching* of the skinny farmers, I don't like a skinny farmer when he *kvetches*: "Look ter me lak we need rain, airp. . . ."

But a flood!

If I wasn't so mean-spirited I would ask God to send your people only good floods.

VAN HORTON Good floods. . . .

FARBER Not that they deserve the pleasure.

VAN HORTON Floods give us pleasure. . . .

FARBER I see already you don't know how to look at a flood.

All right, never mind the advanced stuff. Forget the floating station wagon with the cat on top. And I won't talk variations—where in the current swirls a TV set, the set can be sixteen inches, it can be twenty inches. Or the guy paddling his boat—and the paddle could be a shutter, the paddle could be a storm window.

But back in that gym . . . that town hall!

They pick to interview some bone of a crone . . . a hundred and nineteen.

And what does she say?

With the I-V tubes sticking out her . . . lying on a government surplus cot, covered with a factory reject blanket . . . gumming a day-old doughnut. . . .

What does she say?

"Um real happy, um real glad; um real glad, um real happy."

Why is she so glad and why is she so happy?

"Wal, the real spirit of a town—t'aint in yur greenbean snap-offs. It's frayns an naybees I ain't seen since the last barn-burnin' sharin' their pin-curlers. . . . It's the new young pastor stoppin' by and sayin', 'Hi, we sure missed you at our antifluoride rally.' . . . It's the chance to talk 'bout all them thay-ngs our town's been puttin' off, lak a statue of J. C. Penney, mebbe a new ink pad for Mayor Flang's notary public seal, maybe repaintin' the McDonald's golden arch. . . . Oh, mebbe it's jes plain belongin' . . . sayin', 'This yere's the leech field m'daddy dug.' . . .

'That there's the window fan he won in the Baptist Grand Raffle.' . . . 'The tire chain he used ter teach me right from wrong.' . . ."

VAN HORTON I take away the impression. . . . In my America, amongst my people. . . . Such woefully small expectations.

FARBER Except—and it's a big except—when you deal with your storekeepers.

There you people shine and in that area I acknowledge your superiority.

For your quarter-pound chopped horseneck . . . your filet of fatback . . . your Ma Joad maggot mix. . . .

This sixty-seven cent order . . . it's bagged by a bagger, the bagger throws into the bag five calendars, a copy of *Great Dishes of the Delaware Water Gap*, an ice scraper for the windshield, a bus schedule and a toilet plunger. The stapler staples it with Swedish steel staples, the manager carries it to the car, he apologizes that he can't give your exhaust system a six-point inspection but he just had a couple of disks fused . . . and before he leaves he puts on a little record, the record is John Gielgud going, "Yes, ah, yes, we gladly accept government food stamps. . . ."

VAN HORTON Marx *did* speak of the idiocy of rural life. . . .

FARBER Believe me, it's too good for those idiots. And the street is too good for the man in the street.

VAN HORTON I am at this time tempted . . . no, compelled, I am compelled to say, along with Harry Stack Sullivan, that "most men are much more simply human than anything else."

FARBER Yeah yeah.

Sure sure.

Most men . . . most men are much more simply schmucks than anything else.

VAN HORTON Then what—I put to you Tolstoy's question— what shall a man live by?

FARBER If he can afford it—by the seashore.

VAN HORTON In your tough-mindedness . . . are you not
sometimes afraid of slipping over into plain philistinism?

FARBER Name me a philistine.

VAN HORTON Norman Cousins. Oh, let me not say Norman
Cousins, let me say rather . . . Clifton Fadiman.

FARBER These are your philistines?

Then what should I say about my Uncle Shermie?

Because my Uncle Shermie . . . if I didn't hate under-
statement I would say my Uncle Shermie was the biggest philistine since Goliath. A lug, a lout, a low-life:
He'd see you reading a book, the book could be the
Babylonian Talmud, he'd yell, "Hey! Hey, it's page a
hundred and nineteen!" "What's page a hundred and
nineteen?" "That's where they got the hot parts." If he
went visiting and somebody—it could be the Grand Rabbi
of Jerusalem—somebody said, "May I take your coat?"
he'd answer either "I expect to get it back" or "Remember, the change is counted."

I went one time to the movies with him—a western.
With a scene—you know the scene? Morning, first thing
in the morning. The gunslinger gets up. The gunslinger
rubs his beard. The gunslinger takes out his razor. And he
strops his razor, he gives himself a lovely shave and
again he rubs his beard. He rubs his beard and he wipes
his face and he wipes his razor. He finishes wiping the
razor, he takes his coffee pot, he goes to the stream,
he fills the coffee pot with water from the stream, he
collects twigs, with the twigs he makes a fire, on the fire
he makes coffee, he drinks a cup of coffee, he sloshes out
the grinds, he finishes sloshing out the grinds and he
pours himself a second cup, he drinks the second cup—

And my Uncle Shermie yells out, "*Nu, und pishen
darft m'nisht?*"

Which is to say, "So piss already!"

Which is to say, "Life is life."

Which is to say, "Hooray for reality!"

Which is to say, "From being too tough-minded you don't die."

VAN HORTON Then would I be correct to assume that your uncle bestowed upon you the gift of the given world . . . the world in its marvelous materiality.

FARBER Plus an electric shaver for my bar mitzvah.

But when you're right you're right, and Uncle Shermie was my first instructor in reality.

VAN HORTON After him . . . ?

FARBER Mr. and Mrs. Weingrover.

This is when I was eleven and we had a two-family house. They were upstairs, we were downstairs.

And one day a terrible commotion.

On account of the Weingrovers' Noel got chased off Mr. Ringler's stoop.

And the Weingrovers are giving it to Ringler. . . .

"Please realize, object-hungry small-time property owner, that our child is to us a preciously valuable artifact brought up along the lines of strictest permissiveness and vulnerable to traumatizing shock from your negative No. . . ."

Mr. Ringer answers them, "People . . .

"Please people, parents, good people, I said to the little fellow, what I say to him . . . ? 'Sonny, you have to do bouncy-bouncy with your ball on my stoop at five-thirty in the earliest morning?' The exact words, so help me God, I shouldn't live to enjoy my senior citizen's discount if I'm talking crap."

Crap!

Mrs. Weingrover right away suffers a hormonal change.

Crap!

Mr. Weingrover roars like a Jewish werewolf.

Crap!

"In front of mine wife the harpsichord major you use such usage? Such venal vernacular and foul fulmination? Return to your ox-cart before I administer on you what medieval chroniclers were prone to call a 'grievous hurt!' "

A day and a night later.

From the upstairs. . . .

"Hotbox! Hungry pussy! Get that snatchytwat ready for my come juice, start beating the pillow with your ass, you cunt, beg bitch, beg for my three-and-a-half inch ramrod!"

I laughed.

Yeah yeah.

Sure sure.

I laughed!

VAN HORTON But you don't laugh now.

FARBER Ah, look, maybe they knew what was good.

VAN HORTON This would have pleased D. H. Lawrence.

FARBER Don't start in on me with Lawrence—with the earth's natural rhythms, with the shameful little secrets. Because that stuff—when I was thirteen I knew already.

How did I know?

Baby-sitting.

From baby-sitting I learned human nature and conduct, the psychopathology of everyday life, the origin of the family, the pursuit of the pleasure principle and where they hide the hot books.

I'd walk in a house, I'd look in the bookcase and in the bookcase . . . Crusade in Europe, Lust for Life, God Is My Co-Pilot, The Collected Works of Rudyard Kipling, the first two volumes from the Encyclopedia Schlock. . . .

But in those chests of drawers—under the box of Macy's hard-milled soap and the wedding album and the Our Baby, How He Grew . . .

Fancy My Tickle, Feather My Whip, She'll Be Coming like a Fountain, Show and Swell, When Irish Thighs Are Smilin'. . . .

And I realized two things.

Thing number one is why we're called People of the Book.

But thing number two. . . . Thing number two is the

whole secret of Jewish survival: Keep your sex dirty and your house clean.

VAN HORTON Your attitude toward sexuality . . . I must say . . . that I don't understand, apprehend fully your emphasis on the sordid and sneaky.

FARBER You'll tell me sex is natural, it's lovely and lyrical, it's lyrical and lovely and natural, from there you'll go to communication and fulfillment, how it's the fulfillment of communication, how if you want to get you have to give because the giving is the getting. Right? Am I right?

Only I need you to tell me?

I can hear this from Pat Nixon.

If I said to her, "Hey, Pat, the truth, me you can tell the truth: What do you look for from a *shtupp?*"

"Something more than a *shtupp*, even a good *shtupp*— and the President *shtupps* good. Like, you know, it's Kahlil Gibran and Rod McKuen and Van Gogh sunflowers and the water fountain at Lincoln Center . . . like, you know, it's grooving on the New York Thruway . . . like, you know, man, it's Bobby Fischer's end game and Thomas Aquinas quoting from William Buckley and Bella Abzug buying two-and-a-half pounds of the best flanken. . . ."

And not only Pat Nixon.

Because every carhop and every checkout girl and every chippy and every cellar-club thumper is Molly Bloom and Madeline Herzog.

They want—what don't they want!

Cosmic Man and Noble Savage.

Debasement, but it should be also exalting.

The Story of O as told to Alyosha Karamazov.

Sam Spade and Spade Sam. Popeye with his corn cob, Orpheus with his lute.

No more fuck and suck. Forget fuck and suck. Now it's meaningful dialogue. Meaningful dialogue? Flash cards! "Hello - Lost - Modern - Woman - Who - Has -

Not - Yet - Resolved - The - Identity - Crisis - Of - Our -
Time!" "Hello, hello Post - Dionysian - Man - Swept - Up -
In - The - Neo - Romantic - Agony . . . !"

Maybe it's my training.

Because I got trained good.

By Irma Blatgreen.

Irma, Irma! What are you doing now, where are you,
broken-down Brooklyn College girl?

Irma, Irma, Vocational adviser and social investigator
to the universe.

Live and be well and until the Messiah your heels
should break, your copper bracelets should tarnish, your
shoulder bags should bulge from New School bulletins,
your barrettes should fall off your seven hairs, your fountain should be dry but your elbows smudged with ink. . . .

All right, I'm not saying she didn't give me a little bit
of a hard time or she didn't make demands. Before she
put out you had to sign a petition, cry from at least
three of the six songs for democracy and, to keep up her
spirits, spring for a couple slices of Neapolitan pizza or
a twenty-nine cent "*Guernica*" reproduction.

Only once you *shlepped* her up, up those eleven flights
and into a cold-water flat, once you lighted that half-a-
candle in the wine bottle, once you put Richard Dyer-
Bennett on the record player, once you told her what
was playing next week at the Museum of Modern Art
Film Theater it was all horse and no talk.

"Irma, darling, darling, oh darling, can you take me, are
you ready for me now?"

"No, I'm waiting to get checked-in at Camp Tami-
ment."

Believe me if I tell you that with her a back-skuttle was
love play.

So why did we break up?

On account of one time the ashtrays are on our bellies
and I start in, "Darling, ah darling, talk to me darling
darling, tell me, ah tell me if it was . . . good for you."

"Boy," she answers, "this room could use a paint job."

"Darling darling, the earth, did the earth, darling, move under you?"

"This room?" she goes. "This whole *apartment* could use a first-class paint job."

I got up, I gave back her library card and my last words were, "I'm getting up, I'm giving back your library card and these are my last words."

Irma, Irma, forgive, forgive!

Irma, Irma, you were a day older in wisdom than me. You didn't know much, but what you knew you knew.

Because an orgasm is only an orgasm, but a first-class paint job is good for three years!

VAN HORTON This Irma . . . I just, heh, heh, wonder if she had a sibling . . . slightly, oh, somewhat wall-eyed though otherwise attractive . . . said sibling might have then been studying library science, library science and comparative literature at . . .

Here Ends The First Tape

On the road with Farber to see
I Am a Fugitive From a Chain Gang and The Ox-Bow
Incident at the Commodore Theater, Palm Springs

. . . and Pop says, "Okay kiddo, in any way I can I'll help you, I'm at your service."

So I explain the project.

The project is a civics project and you have to show different examples from your own family of how when social injustice is in the saddle everybody gets a lousy ride.

And I start with the Scottsboro Boys.

"In what way did the Scottsboro Boys case personally show you, in your own life, that no man is an island and cannot enjoy fully his democratic benefits?"

"Kiddo, the Scottsboro Boys. . . . Who can forget that time, that terrible time? I was then looking for a good buy in Rockaway lots and the day they were convicted was the day the lawyer calls me up with just the right price. Oh, I let him have it, I gave him good, I told him on such a black day you have in your mind such crap! He had to call, he didn't have brains enough to slap down a binder immediately and on his own!"

How about Sacco and Vanzetti?

"Also a bad time, kiddo, a worse time even than the Scottsboro Boys. When they were electrocuted your Uncle Shermie and me were so fed up, so disgusted we started to shut the shop for the day. Another minute, in fact, we would have been on the elevator and goodbye forever to the Montgomery Ward order; they sent two telegrams, that's how badly they wanted the fourteen thousand items."

And Tom Mooney?

"Who can ever forget Tom Mooney? During the Tom Mooney tragedy your pop couldn't give enough to his defense fund. What I gave I don't remember but I remember I had it to give; this must've been when the whole world was begging for velvets, they couldn't get enough velvets. . . ."

With Farber at Café Zuckerman, Beverly Hills

We'd be in the street and one Italian kid would yell over, "Hey, ya know what fondalamatzofilleygoo means?" If I answered back even "Nah" my mom was immediately pulling on me. "Jules, lower your voice, look away and turn away, Jules you don't have his racial heritage of leafy vegetable eating, your occasional radish and cucumber is no match for his diet of the finest greens only, Jules we are not as an ethnic group built to be strong-arm *shtarkes*, from our meat cuts we do not obtain the strength they obtain from their meat cuts, even our cheeses come from over-protected cows, compare their whole-milk mozzarella to our Velveeta. . . ." It ended up that the only one she'd let me raise hands against was my pop.

With Farber at the frozen food section
of Max's Rotisserie, Brentwood

There was a time . . . even in my time we had these beautiful, magnificent, tough, capable little Jewish ladies. Ring their bells and they came clopping in felt slippers and housedresses to wash down a corpse, to sit all night on wooden folding chairs and give it an argument for dying, to move the chifforobe so it shouldn't get scratched by the coffin, to clean the house, to fill the refrigerator, to call the obit into the *Jewish Daily Forward,* to tell the son he's a double-breasted louse for never visiting, to spit in the daughter-in-law's face because even when the son wanted she wouldn't let him visit. . . .

Now . . . now they're enjoying shuffleboard days and canasta nights in the condominiums. You can go among them leaking blood and bile, passing kidney stones, arteries hardening, bones softening, balls busting, belly distended, showing boils and cysts and fistulas, swallowing your tongue and digesting your pancreas and swimming in cancer and . . . and they look at you over the aluminum reflectors and they say, "Believe me, you're not doing yourself any good, you should develop more internal resources because mental health is all in the mind, like they say in *Reader's Digest* one green thought drives out ten black ones, and do me a favor, next time they deliver by you oxygen in the tank tell the truckman he'll have big trouble if he parks again in my special reserved parking spot 14-C. . . ."

VAN HORTON . . . did you arrive at the realization that you were different from most other stand-up comics?

FARBER Right after I got kicked by the Twin Cantors and I had to limp on both legs.

Actually . . . actually it had to be when I was working Fendabenda Lodge. My first chance at a second-sitting crowd. . . .

The waiters have cleared the floor, the women are filling their silver purses with black olives and green mints and the manager comes out.

"Lazygenitalmen, welcome to the diamond of the Poconos in a strictly kosher setting and you ever see in your life such *Simchas Torah* sunshine? You happy with the whitefish and how wonderful things are going for Israel? Before I forget let me remind you how on every table is a special creamer for strictly Orthodox guests brimming with purely vegetarian Neo-Lacto entirely without no drop of milky content. . . ."

And the emcee:

"Lazygenitalmen, my first impression will be Jan Peerce doing an impression of Jimmy Cagney. . . .

" '*Eli Eli*, you dirty rat you!'

"My next impression will be Harry Belafonte doing an impression of James Cagney. . . .

" '*Hava Nagila*, you dirty rat, you!' "

And the emcee introduces the vocalist.

"Lazygenitalmen, Phronsie Plotkin, she's gonna do the 'Catskill Lament,' you don't know what is a lament, it's what your wife does when you take off your gotkiss. . . ."

And she sings,

"Wal, I had this room on the American plan,
Nineteen-fifty a day jes to get me a man,
Wal, I painted my toes, wal I smeared on Pond's,
When a voice cried 'Ah work for Israel Bonds.' . . ."

And the emcee is back for his Guess Who impressions.

"Pet-er Pet-er Pet-er Pet-er!"

Guess who?

Bette Davis giving four *goyim* the definition of *putz*.

And the emcee brings out Chick Wing, the top banana. Right away it's "What does a Jewish queer tell his doctor?" Pause. "*Oi*, doctor, have I got a boy for you!" Pause. "Three rabbis are in the Negev watching the irrigation what's making the Israeli deserts bloom when all of a sudden they get the realization that if they don't find soon a potty they'll make in their pants tehhehheh-numbertwo. By circumstantial coincidence a fund raiser from United Jewish Appeal, God bless it, drives by, and in his car is Chaim Weizmann, David Ben-Gurion and Rabbi Stephen S. Wise who also have to make without no delay kahkahlooloo. They knock on the door of the first house they see, a house in which resides . . . Martin Buber. . . ."

And the manager is back.

"Lazygenitalmen, you ever see in your life lower prices and bigger portions? I've been asked for a What's Doing rundown on the upcoming *Rosh Hashanah* calendar of events. You'll be happy, you'll be glad to hear how in the kitchen will be Chef Iz Steingluck, at the shofar will be Cantor Morton Dorton. To answer your many inquiring questions about the constituent ingredients of our whipped cream topping, it's a special secret Fendabenda blend from lima bean, pearl barley and kasha juice. . . ."

Then the emcee; he has another Guess Who.

"Miss-tah Christian! Miss-tah Christian! Miss-tah Christian!"

It's an Israeli sniper complaining.

Finally, finally. . . .

"Lazygenitalmen, let's hear it for Julie Farber, a kid with a friskee piskee, you'll *kvell* how swell and you'll *cholish* from his polish. . . ."

I start with a snappy "*Shalom!*"

I follow up with a "*Chaverim!*"

I ask all newlyweds to kiss and while they kiss I go, "Mazel-tov, mazel-tov. . . ."

And the manager goes, "Off!"

"Off?"

"Off!"

And the emcee fills in with a few bars of "*Que pasa with Hadassah*," he does a Menasha Skulnik tribute, a Yetta Zwerling medley. . . .

While I ask the manager, "Is it my delivery?

"My timing? My pace?"

"Timing and pace I wouldn't want better. But unfortunately and unhappily your comedical routine has a total lackage of the quality I continually strive to give our Fendabenda shows. On this quality I could talk for hours, but I'll sum up in one word: Universality!"

VAN HORTON I take it—and I hope I am so meant to take it—that the tale is apocryphal.

FARBER You know the Myron Cohen line . . . ? Dick Cavett says to him, "Well, that story sounds apocryphal." And Cohen goes, "I never tell Polish jokes."

VAN HORTON Even as you have insisted to Rex Reed, to Judy Klemesrud, to *Playboy* that you never tell Jewish jokes.

FARBER I tell Jewish life in America; that's enough of a joke.

VAN HORTON Isn't that what so many—some would say *too* many—writers have been doing? Painting on the face of the imaginary Jew what Ezra Pound calls "the image of our accelerated grimace"?

FARBER Who needs the imaginary Jew?

Believe me, the real Jew is beyond my imagination.

You want to talk contemporary Jewish life? Here, I'll give you some contemporary Jewish life. Hot from the horse's behind.

The scene—it is so absolutely commonplace I'm ashamed.

Miami Beach.

Gross Miami Beach! Grubby and garish Miami Beach!

But secure—Theodore Herzl never dreamed such security!

And I'm in the A&P.

Where I notice one of Mom's friends.

Mrs. Bimswanger, who once a week reviews books of Jewish content in the clubhouse.

Mrs. Bimswanger, who in her third menopause keeps up with the Israeli Air Force exercises.

Mrs. Bimswanger, who is training her myna bird to say, "Never again, never again."

And she's quavering.

In my life I never saw such quavering. Like a werewolf trying to sing "Mein Yiddishe Momma."

"Hello, Julie dear, might I and could I call upon you for a very special favor?"

What was the favor?

Listen to the favor!

"Maybe you'd ask around where they keep the matzo?"

Reality.

This is reality?

People.

These are people?

These are human punch lines from a Henny Youngman dream.

VAN HORTON I find myself somewhat curious . . . oh, let me not say "curious," let me say rather. . . .

FARBER You mean, did I get her the matzo?

VAN HORTON Did you get her the matzo?

FARBER I got her the matzo.

VAN HORTON Ah.

FARBER All my life I've been getting them the matzo.

VAN HORTON Pity?

FARBER Tribute.

VAN HORTON Tribute. . . .

FARBER Their generation is maybe the last generation that will want matzo. That will be even able to pronounce it.

VAN HORTON Despite a Jewish communal structure envied and emulated—

FARBER Despite.

VAN HORTON Notwithstanding the non-book shelves bursting under *Love and Knishes, Recipes to Lick Your Lips Over . . . Don't Make Dirty* coasters . . . calendars where Christmas and Chanukah, Easter and Passover are rendered simply *Them* and *Us*. . . .

FARBER Notwithstanding and never mind.

All right, maybe it's me.

After all, you . . . you're an ambivalence chaser. You have a mind—it's used to boggling. From cheese dip you'll go to "crisis," you'll make connections from nothing to nowhere and then you'll write a . . . a *monograph* to tell where it's at.

You publish but I perish.

Because my frame of reference—

What frame? What reference?

This Jewish scene. . . .

I could be watching it from Dr. Kronkheit's waiting room. While Jerry Lewis directs and Max Lerner squirts seltzer.

Take . . . take the Anglo-Jewish press.

It used to be . . . my mom would send me the *East Flatbush Jewish Chronicle*, I loved it, I looked forward to it.

The classified ads alone!

Ritual Slaughterer wanted; Minimum ten years experience with ducks; Must provide own knives.

Moey the Matchmaker still accepting applications for the Tishabov mating season . . . From Built-Up Shoes to Built-Up Breasts: You'll Look Nice with our Orthopedic Device. . . .

And they would have gossip columns. . . .

Watch for a crackdown by the Union of Orthodox Hebrew Congregations against circumcision rings . . . Heard about town: The Magid of Vilna is a boarder by his wife . . . It's a low-sodium diet for Rabbi Mendel Fendel, noted Cabala scholar . . . A new baby girl at the Hi Lowensteen household. He's the celebrated coffee table manufacturer. Mazel-tov, Hi—and marble-top.

And the editorials. . . .

Complaining how there's not enough Jewish content in the Old Testament . . . An Open Letter to the Supreme Court: We deplore your refusal to review the charges brought by the American Jewish Congress against Harry Belafonte for yelling *"Pisher"* on Eddie Fisher . . . What should a Jewish doctor tell his patients about hiatus hernia? . . . New hope for the Jewish lonely in middle-sized communities. . . .

Now . . . now they're so fair-minded, they have such a long view. Somebody gets a letter bomb—"We are, after all, in the midst of a cultural explosion" . . . In Forest Hills a cross is painted on the Hebrew National delicatessen—this is "A testament to our common Judeo-Christian heritage" . . . A Hasidic rabbi is pistol-whipped on the Metropolitan Avenue Bus—"Living Proof that transit problems in large cities grow daily more acute and agonizing."

Or I put on TV. . . .

A panel: *"Sources of Black Anti-Semitism."*

There's a black poet and there's a Jewish sociologist. How do I know he's the Jewish sociologist? Because he's the only one with a dashiki and an Afro. And the black poet is giving it to him. "Slumlord" . . . "Zionist imperialist" . . . "Fascist pawn" . . . "Exploiter" . . . "Expropriator" . . . "Slave of the State Department" . . . "Cohort of Colonialism." Then he quotes from Stokely Carmichael who's quoting from James Baldwin on how the Jewish liberals robbed him of his black manhood with their Guggenheim grants.

And the Jewish sociologist, this pathetic jargon junkie answers—listen how he answers. . . .

"More, far more central and crucial, crucial and pointed, pointed and pertinent than anything said, said and spoken here is the fact that men of good will have been able to come and reason together."

Or I go to a bar mitzvah.

Where the bar mitzvah boy gets up and reads from the Pentagon Papers. And while the congregation goes "Right on, right on!" he thanks his mother and father for their activities on behalf of Father Berrigan; his special, his particular thanks, though, to his rabbi, who taught him how Janis Joplin died for us all.

VAN HORTON You condemn, I believe you condemn the Jewish liberal . . . who, however soft-centered his liberalism, is only announcing that he too is a child of the enlightenment, that he too is connected with men everywhere.

FARBER My pop used to say: "All men are brothers—only the sisters-in-law keep making trouble between them."

VAN HORTON Nonetheless your father was a socialist. . . .

FARBER I think because it gave him an excuse to read the New York *Daily News.*

"Here, kiddo, in the *News,* which I make it my strict business to never buy, thank God I find it every day on the subway, is insight into how latter-day capitalism in modern America degrades the masses and divides the classes. It's to me interesting and it's to me instructive to bring to bear my socialist insight upon such prostitutes of the pen, I see the iron heel on the American mind, look at Ingrid Bergman without makeup, without makeup she's all nose. . . ."

But I used to love it when his socialist cronies came.

They'd eat a little sponge cake, they'd finish between the nineteen of them half-a-bottle slivovitz and one— one would go. . . .

"Nah!"

And they'd all go, "You said it!"

"Because the way it was—"

"The way it was won't be again."

"We had leaders with qualities. You could say that the leaders of those days had—you know what they had? Leadership qualities!"

"Class and color! Personalities and powerhouses! You take a Morris Hillquit. . . ."

"Hillquit? I'll tell you about Morris Hillquit. Morris Hillquit was . . . a moral nix."

"A moral nix and a shallow thinker. You want a thinker? Eugene V. Debs was a thinker."

"Debs? Debs was a great thinker. A very great thinker and a very great drinker."

"At least he didn't lack charm. You shook the hand of Debs and you were shaking the hand of . . . a charming man. Not like Alexander Kerensky."

"Kerensky? Kerensky I had one name for—Mr. Fish Eye!"

"Talk to Kerensky and you were always conscious of one thing. You're talking to . . . ALEXANDER KE-RENSKY!"

"But with Kerensky you knew where you stood because Kerensky stood by his principles. And if he hadn't stood by his principles he wouldn't have been Kerensky."

"He would have been Abraham Cahan. You know why? Abraham Cahan was Kerensky without the prinples."

And one, one would go, "Giants. Heroes."

And another would go, "Heroic giants."

And then they'd start talking—now it would soon be Norman Thomas's birthday dinner for a change and for a change they'd each be stuck with two tickets.

VAN HORTON Did your father, like many another Jewish so-cialist, have strong Yiddishist tendencies?

FARBER Forget it.

VAN HORTON No memories of a Yiddish language and literature celebrating a lost and loved culture?

FARBER Lost yeah, loved no.

VAN HORTON I had always imagined . . . clung to the notion
that for Jews no Yiddish word is without mystery and
magic . . . simultaneously consecrating and transcending,
fusing sacred and secular. . . .

FARBER Sure sure!

By you and Leo Rosten.

We enter the world yelling 'Oi' and we leave it whim-
pering 'Gevald.' And in between . . . in between we
argue with the Baal-Shem-Tov about whether the All is
in the Everything or the Everything is in the All.

VAN HORTON Still . . . oh, still is there another language that
yields up so many true words in jest . . . so much jest in
so many true words?

FARBER Someday—you know what's going to happen?
They'll make a Yiddish word and nobody will come to
laugh.

Understand, first of all, that to a Jewish kid Yiddish is
the language of sorrow.

He doesn't hear it, he *overhears* it.

Because in a Jewish childhood it's good news English,
bad news Yiddish.

My pop would come home, on each shoulder an NRA
Blue Eagle, and his first word to my mom was "Later!

"Later I'll say what I have to say in Yiddish as I don't
want to spoil the remaining years of the kid's joyous
boyhood, he'll be going soon enough to a manual training vocational school, stick with Yiddish, in Yiddish only,
for the kid's sake, remember he's listening, how do you
say in Yiddish that my small-time entrepreneurial efforts
got shipwrecked in the shoals of capitalism because the
state wouldn't wither away?"

I was trained so that every Yiddish word heralded the
horrendous . . . portended tragedy like a Greek messenger.

Who—who, in fact, needed to hear words?

My mom would get on the phone with my Aunt Pearlie. . . .

"I am freshly returned from the hospital, Pearlie, I have paid a visit to Cousin Ada, I sought out her doctor, I inquired of the doctor his estimate of her prognosis and this is what he told me, Pearlie, in plain and simple parlance, Pearlie, I am quoting it exactly, I'm rendering it literally, these were his words: 'Well, with her and her condition one may only say, safely say, Ep-peppep-pep or Op-pehpehpeh.' Need I tell you, Pearlie, I Did Not Like The Sound Of That!"

And the obligations of Yiddish.

Are you aware, can you grasp how it obligates and implicates?

When I was three I wouldn't kiss my grandma. "Kissie-wissie on grandma!" "Uh-uh." "For grandma who loves you one kussie-wussie!" "Nyo-nyo and nah-nah." "You don't want to kiss . . . THE . . . BUBBEE!"

Or punishment, take punishment.

By you and yours punishment is honest, open, forthright. The worst, the very worst that can happen to you . . . a little flogging, an evisceration, a disemboweling, a few days in the smokehouse.

But we get—do we even know what we get?

Potches, Charmalyers. Booboos. Klops. Shmeissing and *shlagging.*

And our anatomy. . . .

The melancholy of our anatomy.

You have pricks to effect entry . . . to pierce and penetrate. . . . Cocks!. . . . Masculine masterpieces that evoke images of feisty fowls, of fertility and fruition. For us— why not?—a *schlong* is good enough. *Schlong!* A snake, a repugnant reptile on account of whom man fell.

Look, it's bad enough that in Yiddish you can't name a flower or a bird or a tree, that for all nine hundred varieties of dog we have one word: *Hunt!*

But what about our own names?

Names?

Who has names!

Metaphysical statements.

Zeeskayt . . . Neshomah . . . Tateleh . . . Bubeleh . . .
*Mein layben, mein luft, mein gezunt, mein kraft, mein
mazel, mein gedilah!*

In kindergarten I finally found out my name was Jules.

Yeah yeah.

Sure sure.

Our Yiddish. I tell you our colorful, our cute little
Yiddish will do us in yet.

Why, why do you think we're not making it with the
Third World?

Because even *they* hear things. Even *they* talk.

"Hey, Mistuh Pres,' when yo severin' wid Is-roy-al?"

"Wuffo, man? Dat Is-roy-al jus build us a gen-wine
comm-u-nity college."

"Wuffo? Conner Is-roy-al get bread fum de New Yawk
Hebrew tribe."

"New Yawk? Wea dat be?"

"Dat wea re-side de Jinsberg family."

"Said Jinsbergs be de Jinsbergs fo who mah ahntie
wuk?"

"De same."

"Said Jinsbergs wut lay on mah ahntie sotto voce vilifi-
cation ob contemptible contumely?"

"Contemptible contumely an' odious opprobrium."

"Said Jinsbergs wut all de time be mutterin' on her in
mamalushin tongue."

"Unh-hunh."

"Well man, yo tell dat Is-roy-al ambassador he best
tear-ass over. Cawse efen he *shlepp* . . ."

"Efen he *shlepp* . . . ?"

"Den he gwine know de meaning ob *tsooris*. . . ."

VAN HORTON I had meant at this time to talk of other matters. But throughout . . . given the tone and temper of
your remarks about blacks I must ask . . . this . . . this.

Am I right to believe that you, like many another of my Jewish friends, regard black anti-Semitism with a special, a surpassing sense of bitterness and outrage and blind disgust?

FARBER You mean . . . you mean from everybody else it's history, from them it's *hutzpah*.

VAN HORTON I would not have put it that way, but . . . very well. In fact, yes, definitely yes.

FARBER And it's not only *hutzpah*, it's also a question of gratitude.

Because what we did for those people we didn't do for the rest of the world.

After all, what did we give the rest of the world? Moses, monotheism, maybe a taste for Chinese food.

But them. . . .

Why from my building alone.

The Friday afternoon take-home brigade. . . .

Olivia and Mary and Louise and Mattie and Dorothea clumping to the bus stop, a mural of happy humankind as they heft their shopping bags.

And each shopping bag spills over with testaments of the love our mothers bore them.

"Olivia, oh Olivia honey, oh Mary, oh Louise, oh Mattie, oh Dorothea, be our guest, enjoy, tear in good health these spring coats, these wedgies, these half-slips, these fur-lined gloves, these galoshes, these nighties, and take a chance, try on your Tom, your Earl, your Nola, your Woodrow, your Myrna these slacks and sport jackets and sweater sets and skirts; see, the cleaners' tags are still on them, the original boxes haven't been opened, the tissue is fresh; do me a favor by taking them, I consider it a favor, you're making me happy, make me happy. . . ."

All right, you'll tell me it was patronizing.

VAN HORTON It was.

FARBER You'll tell me we did their pride a terrible injury.

VAN HORTON So you did.

FARBER And still, still I think we're entitled to one thing from them.

VAN HORTON An end to ideology . . . with its triumphant righteousness, its ineffable vulgarity and murderous abstraction.

FARBER That too, that too. But more important, let them at least give back the shopping bags.

Here Ends The Second Tape

With Farber in Fastenberg's
French Cleaners, Malibu

Rabbi Don we had to call him.

And probably Rabbi Don was the world's first relevant rabbi. He was way, way ahead of his time; when the millennium comes he'll be ahead of that time too.

But from him you learned.

You'd say, "Rabbi Don, how come, how is it they write in here that a Jewish person should try to be the tail of a lion instead of the head of a jackal?"

He'd answer, "How come, how is it a gunslinger goes into a saloon, asks for a drink and tells the bartender, 'Leave the bottle?' "

You'd say, "Rabbi Don, why do we have to be so fussy, why do we have to be so particular not to mix dishes?"

He'd answer, "Why is it if a suspect has a perfect motive and his prints are all over and he's without an alibi the assistant to the DA tells his boss it's too pat and it's too perfect?"

You'd say, "Rabbi Don, what's the reason that at a Jewish wedding the groom has to break a glass with his foot?"

He'd answer, "What's the reason all college girls know how to dance so perfectly and one little match lights up a whole castle and nobody looks at a check?"

Then, I forget exactly when, but recently . . . I'm on Forty-second Street, I see him; he's coming out of a real bughouse, the bughouse has *Wetcrotch* and *Return of Wetcrotch*.

I say, "Hello, Rabbi Don. How are you, Rabbi Don?"

I say, "Rabbi Don, what are you doing here?"

And he answers, "What am I doing here? Research!"

VAN HORTON If I consult my impressions I have more than
once caught in your voice throbbings of glory and wonder and danger when you pronounce—no, call up—
Brooklyn and Flatbush. I take the name of Edmund
Wilson less poignantly than you take the name of
Ocean Parkway. As I might speak of E. E. Cummings'
enormous room or Swann's madeleine you speak of Dubrow's cafeteria and Mallomars. You manage to arouse
in me contempt—I hope it is no worse than contempt
—for my lackluster past, my well-scrubbed personal
history—

FARBER I know you already; you probably saw stag movies
before I did. . . .

VAN HORTON Why I lately tend to connect more easily
with your boyhood than with mine. . . .

FARBER . . . Only they were really about stags.

VAN HORTON . . . To think continually and covetously of
your best friends. And why should I not? Could there
have been in the ages of man greater prodigies of in-
solence, more talented lyricists of the *lumpen*, craftier
cocksmen—?

FARBER That's how you talk about my friends? All right
—fuck Huck Finn!

VAN HORTON You've so pumped me up. . . . Really! I've
become so preoccupied with these intellectual gangsters, your Arnies, your Willies, your Milties, your Her-
bies, your Isaacs . . . and by the way . . . by the way I
refuse absolutely to believe Stanley Bloom—is it Stanley
Bloom?—edited, you said *edited* a Trotskyist magazine
at fifteen. . . .

FARBER So I'm a little off. So he had a Flag Day poem in
Senior Scholastic.

VAN HORTON Shall I say I'm drawn to them? I confess; I'm
drawn to them, at least to my conception of them. I
fancy myself in those cellar clubs, those candy stores,
those street corners, a bit more robust and vital than in
life, exulting in that, ah, sensual freedom. . . .

FARBER From our chicks we never took "No" for an answer. "Hey, Norma, you wanna fuck?" "No!" "That's an answer . . . ?"

VAN HORTON What perturbs me . . . the point I'm pressing toward. . . . Perhaps this may not strike you as it struck me, but I have the uneasy impression that the valuation I set on your contemporaries is higher than the one you set, that I at my far remove am less estranged from them, that as I enjoy a kind of secondhand sentimentality you suffer pangs of alienation.

FARBER You're so smart, you're so astute!

VAN HORTON My situation is not without precedent. . . .

FARBER I would twist your nuts, only you'd think it's Living Theater.

VAN HORTON As my former colleague, Pincus Bernstein, observed: "Fellow travelers make the most ardent Bolsheviks. . . ."

FARBER What should I say? Should I say you can't go home again? You can go, but rents are sky-high.

VAN HORTON What I want is some sense of your friends as . . . not as phantoms swirling up from dreamland or Jacobean humors but as elements in your fate—your fate, incidentally, not mine.

FARBER You mean, do I see my old friends?

VAN HORTON Do you?

FARBER I see old movies, I see old friends—and you'd be surprised how sometimes the old movies hold up.

Here . . . !

Two years ago, the kiss-a-pinkie truth, I'm walking past Erasmus Hall and I'm all of a sudden freaking out on memory. Filled up, swelling from fraternity, humanity, loving peace. Ah ah ah! Wowee wowee! Once and for all I'll look him up—Arnie Melitzer with whom I mixed Chinese dishes and traded masturbation fantasies. For him I'll rebuild Steeplechase, the Laffmovie, the Paramount, I'll hire the Norman Luboff choir to sing under his window "Lulu Had a Baby." God willing Arnie has a son, maybe the kid's getting bar mitzvah . . . I'll spring for the affair, I'll send fountain pens and stamp albums in the name of Jeanne Crain and Ann Rutherford and Frances Dee and Bonita Granville. . . .

Then, while the happy tears are still drying, while I'm feeling benign as a tumor, I'm hailed by a hearty "Hello, schmuck-o."

Who is it?

Hershey Shmollowitz.

With his sharkmouth wife—a Mrs. Kenhear. You know Mrs. Kenhear? I can be doing a club date in Syracuse, I can be doing a club date in Fargo and she from the front table is going, "Ken hear! Ken hear! Ken hear!"

And he introduces me. "This, honey, is the Jules Farber I told you about, you remember I told you how I could always beat him in stickball?"

"Oh yuh," she says. "When Ronnie was born we sent him three announcements but we never got a gift."

Then she starts warming up to me: She'd love to say "Come for coffee" but she has to address thank-you cards to the seven-hundred-and-ninety-six people who sent Ronnie such lovely gifts from as far away as Paramus, New Jersey.

And Hershey is explaining that the real reason he never wanted me for recording secretary of the Mohicans was on account of my lousy stickball. Also I was too wild to suit his mother; I'd walk into his house and first thing —first thing!—I used to turn on the radio.

Begins then a byplay. . . .

"Getting enough of it, schmuck-o?"

I'm trying to answer but he keeps backhanding my crotch.

"Oh, I know you got married. . . ."

"What does that mean?" says the wife. "That means a lot. How many of them marry and even have children? Morton Hunt goes into it. . . ."

"Schmuck-o, I was happy you got married. Because I remember in junior high . . . till you got hair on it. . . ."

But the wife is pulling and pulling him, she has to make the stationery store before it closes, to be on the safe side she should pick up another hundred thank-you cards. They walk off and Hershey is yelling how he never saw anybody so bad at stickball, it was my timing, timing is something you're born with, you have it or you don't have it, in stickball and in show business, you take Morey Amsterdam, he has it. . . .

Then last spring he sends me his Temple *Bulletin* and there's an item—it's circled in three colors: *We mourn the loss of Arnold G. Melitzer, who as past chairman of our building fund . . .*

VAN HORTON Your Hershey . . . so much unlove. He would do nicely in my committee room.

FARBER It's worse when they love you.

VAN HORTON "*For this is true and sad, that I need them and they need me. . . .*"

FARBER Did you ever have a couple, and this couple . . . your first couple?

VAN HORTON I daresay.

FARBER But do you know—could you know what I mean by a first couple?

VAN HORTON Those . . . The Ones . . . That Pair . . . as perhaps thesis is to antithesis. . . .

FARBER First Movie . . . First Lay . . . First Death . . . First Couple. . . .

VAN HORTON Those fixed points against which one measures one's life.

FARBER And you never lose touch with them; you never really make contact but never really want to lose touch.

VAN HORTON With mine there was true rapport . . . still is, for my part.

FARBER Every year they send a fifteen cent UNESCO card, and the card has one word—

VAN HORTON I phone mine each Bloomsday.

FARBER —*Hi.*

VAN HORTON Big splendid people; the sour doughbread and Land Rover sort.

FARBER I dream about dropping them, I'm dying to drop them!

VAN HORTON Even as I am tempted to remove her paintings from my den, his anthology from my reading list.

FARBER Last summer I even tried.

Listen how I tried.

I go see my sister, my sister has already a message from them: Tell Julie we are holding open for him the period between July 1 and October 30, during which time he will find visitation quite convenient as we have moved from Far Rockaway to the Kensington Arms two avenue blocks away. While it is a safe building on a safe street we want him to sleep over if he feels like it; this would be absolutely no imposition as we finally have a very spacious junior three-and-a-half apartment.

Now, can you go to a new house without bringing something?

I'll bring them something.

Listen what I bring.

A bottle of wine: Châteauneuf du Sneaky Pete.

Ninety-seven cents; the crest is two green bananas crossed over a field of garbanzo beans.

"This is for us?"

"That one's for you, the Armagnac is for me."

"Ooh, Polly. . . ."

"Ooh, Jack. . . ."

"I think, Polly, that this is the wine . . . this wine got a mention in *Consumer's Bulletin*."

And I have to go with them to the kitchen, I have to see how they chill the bottle, the glasses, their hands.

"Tell me, Julie, if something in this kitchen looks familiar. That something also is a present, a certain present you gave us in Far Rockaway."

You want to hear the present?

I'll tell you the present.

A hunk, a chunk of cork.

"See how we use it? We find it . . . very useful. You take this week alone. Well, this week alone we have tacked on it the FM radio listing and the schedule for the Museum of Modern Art and what's doing at the Ninety-second Street Y and the new and recommended books from the Sunday *Times* and the Brooklyn College concert series and the Art Students League Bulletin, Polly might take a little sculpture, and when I'm supposed to bring the car in for the checkup. . . ."

Then Polly looks at Jack.

And Jack looks at Polly.

"Polly, I am thinking . . . should we all go into the living room, Polly. Who wants to go into the living room?"

And in the living room Jack says, "Well . . . it's a living room."

"Jack, didn't it look bigger on the floor plan?"

"You know Polly, you are right. On the floor plan it looked . . . somewhat bigger."

Then Polly holds out a bowl of shrimps.

And Jack holds out a toothpick.

While they peep and beam at me.

With benevolence.

Benevolence and acceptance.

Acceptance and submission.

Then Polly gives a little tug on my tie.

And Jack brushes my lapels.

We do the "Why did you end up in California?" / "They told me I had a call from the coast, I thought it was Coney Island."

We do the "What is happening with you?" / "I turned down the Nobel Prize so I shouldn't have to *schlepp* to Sweden."

We do the "How do your parents pass the time in Miami?" / "They talk about their favorite states: the state of health and the state of Israel."

We do the "What are the doctors saying about Mitchell?" / "They're talking wolfbane and silver bullets."

Then Polly brings the espresso.

And Jack brings the lemon peel.

While they tell me things, Jack and Polly things.

They have an accumulation of nine days annual leave
plus three days sick leave which they could use either for
the Berkshire Festival and Bear Mountain or Montauk
Point and Cape Cod . . . They are seriously considering
joining a health club or at least going once a week to a
pool . . . They were recently going through the closets
and came across Volume One, Number One of *PM* . . .
They actually started making their own yogurt . . . They
and the Krugmans are thinking of buying a little land
together near Rutland, Vermont . . . They might take a
course together, either "The Literature of Crisis" at
the New School or "Meet Your Car" at P.S. 205. . . .

Then Polly clears away the coffee table.

And Jack brings the photo album.

"This is when we went to see *Potemkin*" . . . "This is
Julie and I when we were busing at Mazur's Manor House;
look how much hair I had" . . . "This, I think, has to
be our wedding reception; you are whispering to Polly
that she shouldn't be the brute her mother was" . . .
"This one, it says the Harriman Park picnic; *oi* till you
got the fire going" . . . "This I wonder who took, unless
it was Mutzey Fromberg; we all ended up in the Village
and you nearly got us killed by a bunch of lesbians" . . .
"This one you're helping us move into Perry Street;
look how he's helping, he's carrying one book. . . ."

Then Polly says, "Ah, are you looking at your watch?"

And Jack says, "What are you looking at your watch?"

Then Polly shows how the couch converts to a three-
quarter bed.

And Jack shows me that the pillow is a nonallergenic
pillow.

"Sleep over," they're begging.

And *Sleep over*, says the Modigliani print.

Maybe you should sleep over, says the bullfight poster.

You could sleep over, says the Japanese wind-bell.

Why can't you sleep over? say the brick and board book shelves with the eleven Modern Library giants and the boxed Proust.

So I figured, Can it hurt?

Even if it does hurt. . . .

After all, you'd have to have the heart of a murderer or a High Episcopalian.

And I started to realize such a truth, oh wowee, such a marvelous marvelous truth. . . .

VAN HORTON Perhaps the same truth I find in Isaac Rosenfeld's plea: "Be gentle to the unfulfilled."

FARBER That and also how I hinted one little hint I would get salami and eggs in the morning.

Here Ends The Third Tape

With Farber at The Candybox, Sunset Boulevard

She'll be elected—a landslide!

And she'll call in her cabinet, they'll confer—an hour, two hours. Then . . . then they'll make pursy little mouths, they'll go all together to the bathroom, in the bathroom they'll comb each other's hair and while they comb each other's hair. . . .

"I really should go soon for A Thorough Internal Examination."

"Darling, don't neglect it."

"Sure I shouldn't neglect it. Only who'll attend the NATO meeting and who'll deal with the Common Market and who'll sign the trade pacts where each pact you have to sign fifty times!"

"Darling, health comes first; you want a favorable balance of trade or a favorable report on your Pap smear?"

"Believe me, you are so right. Because the way I'm killing myself for this country. . . . You I can tell: Last week in Camp David I had . . . such discomfort, such cramps that I was embarrassed for Golda."

"Did you give her the jets?"

"Look, could I tell her 'No'? After all, she finally gave me the name of her own GYN man. . . ."

VAN HORTON Other than your neighborhood nymphomaniacs—

FARBER I never laid a girl from the neighborhood. They had to live at least three blocks away—avenue blocks!

VAN HORTON —Are there no women you admire?

FARBER He refuses to understand how I'm crazy about pussy!

Try to believe me if I tell you I love pussy; all right, I'd love it better if there wasn't a woman attached.

VAN HORTON The New Woman clamoring for her place, her rightful place in the sexologist's Heavenly City.

FARBER Then give her the place already.

She can have even my place, let her stop the clamor.

Because I can't take it any more.

I mean . . . every *yenta* is a mentor.

And a dissenter. . . .

"Mine Hymie wants only I should give him for breakfast belly lox. You hear? Belly lox he wants, that King of Lovers! You know when he'll get belly lox? When he breaks the emotional tension of mine dammed-up erotic hunger—and I'm not talking no cockamamy clitoral climax; clitoral climax I can get from the slipcovers. Let him only cut out the *ejaculatio praecox* and I would show that little *shvantz* a response—I'd be by him an Earth Mother, a partner in passion, a pleasure garden and believe me, I wouldn't even wear mine corset in bed. . . ."

VAN HORTON If Desdemona had read Masters and Johnson how much sooner would Othello have strangled her.

FARBER And while she's dying she'd tell him "Between consenting adults everything is permissible."

VAN HORTON Or as I was lately reminded by a colleague: "An aperture is an aperture." Quite a gifted poetess . . . had her down for a year . . . one might say as the, heh heh, writher-in-residence.

FARBER There was a time. . . . It used to be you'd be bang-

ing a broad, you'd finish up and you could make real
contact. . . .

VAN HORTON Quite a decent piece of ass . . . although somewhat given over to the technical side of things.

FARBER "Come. If you love me you'll come. Come if you
love me. I love it when you come. When you come I
love it better than when I come and you know how I
love to come. But when I love to come I love it because I'm coming with you. . . ."

VAN HORTON Can't say if this is typically Middle-European
but . . . she seemed to regard my, ah, penis as an organ
of the State Department. . . .

FARBER "You think I care about coming? When I come
for myself I'm coming for you. Because if I didn't come
for you you couldn't come for me. And I wouldn't
want you to come just for yourself. . . ."

VAN HORTON "I cannot make a good franz with your preeck.
Your preeck is brute, your preeck is meat, your preeck
is colonialist, your preeck make napalm on in-fant
bay-bees. . . ."

FARBER "Let me make you come. I can make you come.
Come in a rush but don't rush to come. Take your time
and come. Come, take your time. What can I do to
make you come? Tell me if you can come but come
without telling me. . . ."

VAN HORTON " 'Allo, Meester Preeck. Where are you going,
Meester Preeck? March tall, leetle sol-jer, tomorrow
brings time to move on peasant village. . . ."

FARBER "Sure you came. Don't you know if you came?
Believe me, you came. You acted like you came. I think
you came. You think too much about coming. . . ."

VAN HORTON "Tell me, Meester Preeck, 'ow many trees you
defoliated today an' 'ow big shall be our nuclear de-
terrent?"

FARBER "What then, I wouldn't see you in the city? Sure
I'll see you in the city. I know exactly where you live

in the city. I'm writing it all down, see how I'm writing it down. In the city . . . Lorraine Levy. . . ."

VAN HORTON I pressed strongly for her reappointment but . . . she and the chairman failed to find the elements of common discourse.

FARBER "That's T,H,E . . . That's C,I,T,Y. . . ."

VAN HORTON She went about calling him "Teabag" and "Drip-dry."

FARBER Yeah yeah.

Sure sure.

What I looked for then . . . forget what I looked for then.

Now I'll grab somebody who can put stability in my life and bowls of Jell-O in my refrigerator.

VAN HORTON "I could have forgiven her excesses," he confided to me over a bottle of dry sack, "her whispering campaign about my doctoral dissertation . . . 'Myth and Symbol in Our College Medical Plan' indeed!"

FARBER The Jell-O should have in it crumpled walnuts—crumpled, not chopped.

VAN HORTON She did, I suppose, go out of her way to slip him the old needle. I think particularly of the time the Academic Senate was deadlocked in its efforts to agree on a strongly worded statement showing our concern for both consumer protection and civil rights. Well, she took the floor and demanded he read into the record the following: *We support the black man's struggle to eat white pussy that is free of carcinogenic preservatives.*

FARBER A nice middle-class girl. With starched slips and clean brassieres and a crush on Paul Newman. In whose presence all ovens become self-cleaning and laundry sorts itself and leftovers beg for Saran Wrap. A real rebel who never went to her Hunter College graduation. Who three times in her life said "Shit," once in front of her mother.

VAN HORTON I pressed strongly for her reappointment. But . . . no tenure without the old Ph.D.

FARBER Such a one . . . oh, such a one would never lack from dove's milk or tiger's milk. Because I would do for her—what wouldn't I do for her?

VAN HORTON And campus maverick or not, she should have known better than to smoke in the halls.

FARBER I'd bring her along. I'd educate her into a natural child, a true daughter of Israel.

We'd furnish in waxed fruit and sequins.

We'd be active in Jewish affairs, we'd know how to give a plaque and take a plaque.

To visitors we'd mail out hectographed directions: Go past the Lox Wing, the Nosh Bar, and bear right at the Big Fat Salami. You keep Harmony Hall on your left till the blinker at the intersection of Dignity Drive. . . .

I'd come home, she'd be hanging Käthe Kollwitz prints and telling me Harry Golden's at the temple.

We'd talk Chaim Potok and Leon Uris and on Chanukah we'd give each other one-month subscriptions to *Commentary*.

I'd build her a little studio where she could paint by numbers.

She'd say, "Formica," I'd say "Naugahyde."

We'd sit in a matched set of Barcaloungers at the rear of the avant-garde.

It's terrible?

What's so terrible?

VAN HORTON Indeed, indeed . . . if the simple life would have me, I would have the simple life.

FARBER I'm in prime time but my sex life is a summer rerun.

VAN HORTON I too, I too. It's become all *déjà vu* and wanhope and once more unto the breach with Bob Dylan and incense, Marvel Comics and Rod McKuen.

FARBER With their demands . . . you hand them a Kleenex, the Kleenex has to be fresh!

VAN HORTON And the postcoital patter. . . .

FARBER Who listens?

VAN HORTON To hell—I say to hell with Tolkien and Vonnegut! I refuse categorically to lower my standards along with my trousers.

FARBER Because with my nitwit nookie I don't have to listen.

I pull out, I go "Hi" or "Hi, there. . . ."

VAN HORTON I generally have a few lines of verse at the ready.

FARBER I give a little . . . I think it's called a "little shiver of ecstasy." And I say, "Wow. . . ."

VAN HORTON I've had some success with Donne: "*Your eyes give out more light than they take in.* . . ." For those wearing contact lenses I make do with the Lake Poets.

FARBER Then I wait; you have to wait. I count, "One Nitwit Nookie . . . Two Nitwit Nookie . . . Three Nitwit Nookie. . . ."

VAN HORTON At around this time I generally administer . . . I, ah, nip at the old hinterlands. . . .

FARBER By "Five Nitwit Nookie" I start praising their parts. "I love, I am crazy about the pink aureoles of your right breast."

VAN HORTON Without of course drawing blood.

FARBER "And your dusky feminine odors—I can barely wait till dusk!"

VAN HORTON Followed by a merciless pummeling of the posterior. Oh, let me not say "merciless." . . .

FARBER Then I hear "Cultural disorientation." . . .

VAN HORTON Let me say rather "mildly sadistic" or "pleasantly cruel."

FARBER I hear "identity crisis. . . ."

VAN HORTON I get Sylvia Plath.

FARBER I hear "Give" . . . "Love" . . . "Confront" . . . "Feel" . . . "Find" . . . "Dare" . . . "Change" . . . "Become" . . . "Know." . . .

VAN HORTON My last discussed filmic values.

FARBER They want, before it's too late—and already it's getting very late because they've had three walk-ons in *Hawaii Five-O*—

VAN HORTON All torn up—was she true cinéaste or mere movie-buff?

FARBER What don't they want?

VAN HORTON Had she done right in giving up the potter's wheel for the handheld camera?

FARBER To take a different exit ramp.

To blow glass.

To train with guerrillas.

To write a children's book.

To make rain.

To work in a rice field. . . .

VAN HORTON Should she forgive Eisenstein for killing all those horses?

FARBER To be sprayed with Mace.

To smoke a hookah.

To date Senator Fulbright.

To drive a truck with sixteen forward speeds.

To screech at seagulls.

To open a coffeehouse.

To design place mats. . . .

VAN HORTON Did John Huston sell out or cop out?

FARBER To cook bouillabaisse.

To predict an earthquake.

To grow mandrake root.

To make curtains for a VW camper.

To print on a hand press.

To cut sugar cane.

To talk to a porpoise. . . .

VAN HORTON Why is Kubrick lately moving in so close on his close-ups?

FARBER To predict an earthquake.

To be thrown off an army post.

To seal up a missile silo.

To build puppets.

To bind books.

To spend a summer with Bushmen. . . .

VAN HORTON She's now after me to sponsor her for a Guggenheim. . . .

FARBER To make it with Buckminster Fuller.

To skinny-dip with Jacques Cousteau.

To drive a converted hearse with two hundred thousand miles on the odometer.

To save an endangered species.

To plan a city. . . .

VAN HORTON Wouldn't be entirely undeserved . . . the girl, after all, has everything Pauline Kael has.

FARBER To sign a treaty with the Navajos.

To hold a hostage.

To hook a rug. . . .

VAN HORTON Mustache, muscles, broad shoulders. . . .

Here Ends The Fourth Tape

With Farber at Toys 'n' Stuff, Culver City

How I survive I don't know, but we'll say I survive World War III.

And with my Geiger counter I walk uptown and downtown and crosstown.

And while I walk I come out with every one-liner I know, and after the one-liners I sing every song I know, and after the songs I name whatever has a name.

Then through the vapor I'll see him.

And he'll see me.

And we'll walk to each other and we'll touch and feel and pound on each other's backs.

And I'll go, "Wow, oh wowee!"

And he'll go, "Cagney and Robinson played together in one picture and one picture only, and the name of that picture was . . ."

VAN HORTON You have so befuddled and befouled my film sense that I fear to slight the claims of the lowliest Sam Katzman quickie. . . .

FARBER One thing about Sam Katzman: He gave you terrific lap-dissolves!

VAN HORTON Under your training . . . your spell, I find myself picking out, in the biggest crowd scenes, the faces of George E. Stone and Warren Hymer and Nat Pendleton and Stanley Ridges. . . .

FARBER Edward Brophy I don't hear. . .

VAN HORTON And why not? I am pleased; these were, after all, timeless small-timers. All the same I do not especially appreciate . . . I find your arrogance. . . .

FARBER I'm arrogant?

VAN HORTON Your implicit arrogance. . . .

FARBER I'm implicitly arrogant? All right. Okay. Screw you, dumbhead *goy.*

VAN HORTON As though I had never before beheld the light of the screen.

FARBER Without me you'd still be knocking out the dottle from your well-used briar and going, *"Potemkin, Potemkin!"*

VAN HORTON May I say . . . I shall say that well before, *long* before this day I had expressed reservations about the art film!

FARBER He was reading *Peanuts* . . . he was reading *Peanuts* and writing about how *Snoopy* is a doctrinaire liberal.

VAN HORTON Agreed. Accepted. *Nolo contendere.* Once and for all. Now and forever. I acknowledge—and when have I not?—how many of your views I have appropriated. . . . In these matters . . . not only these . . . I have been your disciple.

FARBER Did I bring you along too fast? After all, overnight from Shake 'n' Bake to matzo meal. . . .

VAN HORTON Why then so testy, so touchy? And such disdain! Or is it disdain?—merely disdain.

FARBER Maybe a little contempt.

VAN HORTON I believe you to be threatened. Are you threatened?

FARBER That's what I once asked Don Rickles; I said, "You're even more threatened than me," and he said, "Kid, that's my only security."

VAN HORTON That is a vulgar refutation! That is horseshit! Oh, let me not say "horseshit," let me say rather . . . relative crap. You feel threatened . . . yes, somehow you do, by my news. My pathetic piece of news. Yes, yes, the very moment you heard it is the very moment you began pelting me with salted peanuts.

FARBER Barton's Continental Mixture is not salted peanuts.

VAN HORTON I had thought you might advise me. Who better than you?

FARBER I'll advise you: Don't give the course.

VAN HORTON In the name of God, why not?

FARBER Because there are certain things you don't teach. Because there are certain demands you don't supply.

VAN HORTON My universe has room for Bogart as well as Beowulf.

FARBER You're taking in too many boarders.

VAN HORTON And you should know, you certainly should know that I am a pedagogue, not a panderer. If—and the course is far from finalized—If I deal with Krazy Kat, I shall be no less exacting than I have been with Kafka.

FARBER In you I have confidence. But your students—I piss on all their desks!

VAN HORTON That smacks of rankest youth-baiting. Or is it pathetic pride? Is that it? Do you alone enjoy a life-pass for the midway of mass culture? Are you the by-blow of Blondie and Dagwood?

FARBER I'm only a Flatbush boy who went to the movies. I went to the movies and I read the jokes and I listened to the radio and I did what I had to do—and what I had to do was go to the movies and read the jokes and listen to the radio.

VAN HORTON What of your Mickey Mouse watch?

FARBER It kept lousy time.

VAN HORTON And your Orphan Annie mug? From which you drank . . . Ovaltine.

FARBER The mug chipped in my hands. And the Ovaltine kept me awake.

VAN HORTON Oh now, really. Really! I have seen you. . . . Forgive me, but. . . . The sneaky weeping over Garfield. And Muni. And Raft. . . .

FARBER I'm entitled.

VAN HORTON So are we all.

FARBER Yeah yeah.

Sure sure.

VAN HORTON For me it's *Casablanca*. A certain line—of all lines! "Everybody goes to Rick's." Spoken by Claude Rains.

FARBER Let me give you a better line. "Pay the two dollars . . . Pay the two dollars." Spoken by Willy Howard.

VAN HORTON Ah. Of course.

FARBER Thanks for the "of course." . . .

VAN HORTON That's unworthy of you.

FARBER It's worthy, it's worthy.

VAN HORTON I too am aware that those were dark times. I too have associations. In my nightmares the same faces. . . .

FARBER I believe you.

VAN HORTON So you should.

FARBER So I *have* to.

VAN HORTON Then take your chances with the young—or would you have them also pay the two dollars?

FARBER I don't want they should pay the two dollars.

God forbid they should pay the two dollars.

VAN HORTON They expect to. Ah, how easily they speak of apocalypse.

And with such self-delight . . .!

FARBER Then tell them—you know what you should tell them?

To smell their own vomit.

To play with their own cocks.

To rob their own graves.

But stop—stop, stop, stop already with the nostalgia, the trivia, the camp, the pop. Let the parade go by. . . .

VAN HORTON Which parade would you have them join? Yesterday a student—and one of my better students—complained, lamented, "Man, like all the good causes are taken. . . ."

FARBER He can finish freeing the Rosenbergs.

VAN HORTON As to that . . . I notice Henry Wallace has become something of a Big Man on Campus. Bobby Seale, when he addressed the Students Union, received a smaller fee than Alger Hiss. And I believe, if I'm any judge in these matters, that Che Guevara's corpse is beginning to stink, that the young would have the genuine article—Stalin, the authentic Prince of Darkness.

FARBER Wait.

Wait, wait, *chaver*, it's not over yet.

VAN HORTON They would forgive him the purges and The Pact—

FARBER Everything will be trivia and everything will be nostalgia.

VAN HORTON —If only they knew what the purges and The Pact were.

FARBER The Messiah will come—but you know how he'll come? On the backs of Laurel and Hardy.

VAN HORTON I went about my Comp Lit seminar. . . . Only one in five could give me the year of the Russian Revolution. They confused the New Deal with the New Economic Policy. . . .

FARBER He'll go, "Wanna buy a duck?" He'll go, "Big money in radio!"

VAN HORTON None—I include, I fear, two Jewish students —could define pogrom. . . .

FARBER The concentration camp will be camp. . . .

VAN HORTON This so enraged me—oh, let me not say enraged, let me say rather embittered . . . embittered me that I went to the blackboard. "Human beings do not know that everything is possible." I wrote down. And "Those who do not remember the past are condemned to relive it. . . ."

FARBER An Auschwitz blowup—a *good* Auschwitz blowup —will go for as much as an original *King Kong* poster. . . .

VAN HORTON I found them tittering, sniggering and tittering the next day. Turned around to check my fly . . . saw on the blackboard, though I pretended not to, NOV SHMOZ KA POP and GLORYOSKY, ZERO, I GOT THE WHIM-WHAMS ALL OVER. . . .

Here Ends The Fifth Tape

With Farber at
the Millie and Max Delicatessen, Hollywood

They had this routine, my pop and Uncle Shermie.

My pop would say, "I notice there's going to be a nice sport jacket sale at Harry Rothman's."

My Uncle Shermie would say, "I ordered a Philco 6000 BTU air conditioner from the Friendly Frost store."

My pop would say, "I brought the car in for a lube and the mechanic said I should switch over to a 20-W oil."

My Uncle Shermie would say, "I'm thinking of trying out Hoffritz's own make cordless shaver."

Then my pop would say, "This sport jacket and this air conditioner and this oil and this shaver. . . ."

Then my Uncle Shermie would say, "Are they good for the Jews?"

And they'd go, both together, "Probably not, probably not. . . ."

VAN HORTON Even after all this time?

FARBER It hurts, it hurts.

VAN HORTON But what do you expect? What could you have all along expected? To be seated on a dais?

FARBER At least a table in the kitchen.

VAN HORTON As you have yourself said: "What do you get if you mate with a monkey? A very angry monkey." To which I would add that he who goes about outraging rabbis must not be surprised to have dealings with . . . outraged rabbis.

FARBER From the outraged rabbis I could live.

Live and laugh.

God bless them and give me only the outraged rabbis. Nosepicking old-timers with iron yardsticks and steel-wool beards. Who can tell you to get maimed and butchered and plucked; and also how you shouldn't forget next Tuesday to fast.

But they got kid brothers. And those kid brothers. . . .

Rabbi It-Is-With-A-Heavy-Heart!

Rabbi Let-Us-By-All-Means!

Rabbi Self-Examination-Yes; Self-Hatred-No!

Rabbi Balanced-Representation-Of-American-Jewish-Life!

VAN HORTON It was Spengler, I believe, who prophesied that the hyphenated man would prevail.

FARBER With their open letters. . . .

Dear concerned readers of the Mizrachi Monthly *and* Jews everywhere *in this democratic and pluralist society—*

VAN HORTON Ah, the universal cleric-ese. As though the Spirit of Xerox were to address the Council of Churches.

FARBER *Viewing watchers of the "Mike Douglas Show" are probably still smarting from the stereotyping slander out of the big mouth of Jules Farber, already well-known to readers of these pages for his hostility to such American-Jewish institutions as the Urban League. . . .*

VAN HORTON So we shall be talking—and long before the state withers away.

FARBER I share, along with the vast and overwhelming majority of Americans, Mr. Farber's expressed belief that "It's a good thing we got out of Vietnam." But not, surely not, certainly not because "They got in the North such a terrible big dog!" This statement from the lips of a Jew—at least one who professes Judaism —can be received only with shock and dismay, scorn and contempt. No, Mr. Farber, be assured, sir, that Jewish fear of and hostility toward dogs exists only in your mind and in the mind of bigots and demagogues throughout the ages. Certainly there are, there have always been differences and discord between Jew and dog—but these differences are slowly giving way to what the American Kennel Club has called "a growing realization that each can contribute his full, fair share toward the enrichment of our common Judeo-Christian heritage.

VAN HORTON Perhaps . . . oh, perhaps you ask too much of the rabbis.

FARBER What do I ask?

VAN HORTON That they look out from your window on the world.

FARBER And what would they see?

VAN HORTON A fire escape. I suppose. And on that fire escape would be—ah, "such a terrible big dog."

FARBER Isn't there?

VAN HORTON But the rabbis—and not the rabbis alone— would rather look out upon the American Kennel Club.

FARBER I'm stopping them?

VAN HORTON You're stopping them, you're stopping them.

FARBER I mean harm?

VAN HORTON No more than did Jeremiah. But which Jewish community center has a Jeremiah Room?

FARBER If Jeremiah had been Jerry Lewis he'd have had the whole center.

Plus a laminated illuminated plaque.

"To Jerry Lewis who has given so much of himself; who in the giving has never ceased reminding us 'If you don't give God'll make on you nyeh-nyeh pee-pee shame-shame.'"

But me—it's the Farber fate.

In the beginning was the word, and for Farber the word was *Feh!*

VAN HORTON *Feh* as in expletive or *Feh* as in accusatory . . . ?

FARBER *Feh* as in "Don't shit where you eat."

VAN HORTON Oh you people and your dietary proscriptions!

FARBER *Feh* as in "It don't look good for the *goyim*."

VAN HORTON For us it's good enough.

FARBER *Feh* as in "How come we never hear from you something about Haym Salomon or Jacob Riis or Lester P. Cohen, this was America's first butter-and-egg man, or how we contributed beyond numerical proportion to the opening of the West—"

VAN HORTON —We wanted log cabins, you wanted bungalow colonies. We offered the Indians firewater. . . .

FARBER But the worst *Feh* . . . the *Feh* that smites you hip and thigh . . . the *Feh* that kills is the Vampire *Feh*.

VAN HORTON . . . You offered them fire insurance.

FARBER The Vampire *Feh* goes back, way back to when the family drove up to see me at Fendabenda Lodge.

And I was feeling good.

I figured—why not?—I'll try a new shtick. Famous Scenes From Famous Pictures.

I do wind sounds.

I do storm sounds.

I build up and up to the fearful *gevald* of peasants.

"Scorch him with a torch!" . . . "Bang on his fang!" And over this fearful *gevald* . . .

"Mine Marvin is a vampire? So how is he hurting you? The boy sucks only on Jewish necks . . . he sleeps in a coffin because he *has* to sleep in a coffin; for his slipped disk he needs under him strictly super-firm. . . . Yeah, right away, sure, I'll put stakes in his heart because he goes out at night. What then, he shouldn't go out? This is a grown boy, he should live and be well, he'll be next week twelve hundred. . . ."

And I run over to the family.

"Family, hey, family, you liked it?"

"Lovely," says my Aunt Pearlie. "Lovely, lovely. Except it's not nice for the vampires."

VAN HORTON Even after all this time. . . .

FARBER It hurts, it hurts.

VAN HORTON Joyce said it: "A hundred cares, a tithe of troubles and is there one who understands me?"

FARBER Happens . . . happens there was one.

VAN HORTON And that one . . .?

FARBER Sugarman.

In Buffalo.

Years and years ago I had to do three nights in Buffalo and all three nights he's parked right under my mike. A sweet, a scholarly little man . . . the kind of face only Maimonides could love . . . a smile like he's expecting messages from Heaven. And he's nodding and he's swaying and he's going, "Sugarman understands you, Sugarman understands you. . . ."

On the third night he sends the waiter with an egg cream, he invites me to his table, I sit down and he tells me he wants to interview me.

"Reb Farber, let Sugarman heal the breach between you and the American Jewish community."

Why, Sugarman? How Sugarman?

"Because Sugarman is of your mind and kind. Because Sugarman also gives bear-hugs and is returned buffets. Because Sugarman likewise cries, 'Pox!' and 'Plague!' Because Sugarman digs you and grooves on your message."

Let me hear my message.

"The message is . . . Maybe we survived the Warsaw Ghetto, but be very careful with the Great Neck Open Classroom controversy.

"The message is . . . If you can't keep up with the foot-men, don't race the chariots.

"The message is . . . The Tigris and Euphrates meet, and in Paramus we'll get our feet wet.

"The message is . . . Bad Luck and the Bloomingdale's Accounting Department always know where to find a Jew.

"The message is . . . What's scheduled for urban re-newal? The street they just named after you."

I go, "Wowee."

"Do I get the interview, Reb Farber?"

You get it, you get it.

"So for openers tell Sugarman how long even a Haman like you thinks he'll get away with it; aren't you a little bit afraid of God . . .?"

VAN HORTON Are you?

FARBER What can He do to me?

VAN HORTON He can—how does that joke go?—He can open some big mouth on you.

FARBER You got the wrong God.

VAN HORTON We *goyisher* intellectuals . . . you must realize we love that fear and trembling. That void . . .!

FARBER From that void He moved.

VAN HORTON To be closer to His Mother . . .?

FARBER Now He has a suite.

And you have to make an appointment.

And when I finally get the appointment I'll walk in, I'll say. . . .

"I'll say, "With children you have to be lucky."

He'll answer me—like this He'll answer me: "What, after all, what is luck? As I once told my servant Job, as I more recently reminded the New York School of Social Work, luck is finally, ultimately a function of . . . char-acter. But character, after all, is conditional upon and subject to the factors of environment and heredity."

I'll say, "What's going to be?"

And He'll answer me—like this He'll answer me:

"Well, I have never stopped insisting that the certainties of yesterday are the problems of today, that if mankind is not merely to endure but prevail it must find, perhaps through the agency of the United Nations, perhaps in church and synagogue, some viable means of wedding the best of the old time-honored moral truths to modern scientific advances."

I'll say, "Is there something You could recommend?"

And He'll answer me—like this He'll answer me: "At this point, I fear, our data is still inconclusive, though preliminary findings point toward a universal falloff in relevant goal-aspiration. It remains to be seen whether this falloff derives from an abiding crisis of faith or a temporary decline in what my former colleague, Moses, demanded for Egyptian Jewry—namely, unobstructed vocational mobility."

I'll say, "*When* it happened we know, but how come we don't know exactly *what* happened?"

And He'll answer me—like this He'll answer me: "We would all of us do better to cultivate more positive, more constructive attitudes, at the same time seeking to awaken public interest in supporting, with full and adequate funding, ongoing social welfare programs, programs whose future existence depends upon an aroused citizenry and a concerned government."

I'll say, "If there's only what is, who needs it?"

And He'll answer me—like this He'll answer me: "I have heard similar viewpoints expressed in the past, most notably by Isaiah and Ecclesiastes. To them, to you, I would say this . . . that such outlooks and insights fail to grasp the correspondence between emotional and economic health. You might recall my sampling of attitudes toward poverty amongst strip miners in West Virginia. Well, one of those interviewed spoke doubtlessly for the great bulk and overwhelming majority of his situational peer-group when he said, 'You dig sixteen tons and what do you get? Another day older and deeper in debt. . . .'"

I'll say, "Goodbye, take it easy and maybe . . . maybe next year in Jerusalem."

And He'll answer me—like this He'll answer me: "Right now my plans for the forthcoming year are tentative and uncertain, though you may be assured I wish this gallant little nation all and every success in its efforts to secure a just and lasting peace in the Middle East."

Here Ends The Sixth Tape

With Farber in Rosen's Dairyfood Delights, Brentwood

What then, my pop and I don't talk?

We talk, we talk.

But there's one talk . . . one talk we'll have yet.

I'll start, I'll have to start, "Pop, hey, Pop, are we in the same boat? I mean, still in steerage, still coming to an America? Tell me, me you can tell. . . ."

Then he'll say, "Now you come to me? Why didn't you wait till I was in intensive care? If I'm like every father must you be like every son?"

Then he'll say, "Okay. Okay, kiddo."

Then without stop, like we each had a hundred mouths and each mouth was doing an oral history of the world, the stuff will pour out. And what stuff, what stuff! God and man and Devil; earth and fire and water; flesh and spirit; the wheel and the clock; knives and forks and potties; Sodom and Gomorrah and the growth of the suburbs; Gandhi and Lenin and David Dubinsky; red Volvos and encounter groups and the Pentagon Papers; Ruth and Naomi and retirement villages; Junglegyms and fluoride treatments and permissive upbringing. We'll clear up the Mystery of Mysteries and then . . . then first. . . .

With Mitchell at the Children's Zoo, Bel Air

No No No No No No No No No No No No No No
The Mish do No No No No No No No No No No
Not Not
No No
The Mish do No do No do No do No do No do No
No No No No No No No No No No No No No No

A Note on the Type

The text of this book is set in Electra, a typeface designed by W. A. Dwiggins for the Mergenthaler Linotype Company and first made available in 1935. Electra cannot be classified as either "modern" or "old style." It is not based on any historical model, and hence does not echo any particular period or style of type design. It avoids the extreme contrast between "thick" and "thin" elements that marks most modern faces, and is without eccentricities which catch the eye and interfere with reading. In general, Electra is a simple, readable typeface which attempts to give a feeling of fluidity, power, and speed.

This book was composed, printed, and bound by The Book Press, Brattleboro, Vt. Typography and binding design by Carole Lowenstein.